Jenny 4

Paul Drew

Charleson & Associates ✱ Spring Lake Heights, New Jersey

A Charleson & Associates Book

Published by Charleson & Associates, Spring Lake Heights, NJ 07762

This book is a work of fiction. Names, characters, places, and events are products of the author's imagination. Any resemblance the reader may find to reality is purely coincidental.

Copyright © 2004 by Paul Drew

All rights reserved, including the right to reproduce this work in whole or in part in any form. Published in the United States of America.

Library of Congress Number: 2004105746

ISBN: 0-9754805-0-2

Cover Design by Ryan Feasel

Manufactured in the United States of America

First Edition: 2004

10 9 8 7 6 5 4 3 2 1

Dedication

To The Birthday Club:
Charlie, Honey, and Paschal

Acknowledgments

When I began this work, I chose names that, frankly, were convenient for me to remember, figuring that I would change them along the way as characters took shape, found their place. Some are surnames of guys I served with in the United States Army, some are American Legionnaires, others just sounded right. With a few exceptions, I found no reason to change them. I kept them in respect for their namesakes' honorable service to our country in time of war. There is, however, no connection, express or implied, between the fictional characters in this book and any person, alive or dead.

Language, particularly language that modern readers have unfortunately come to expect in "war" stories, is an issue I did not struggle much about right from the beginning. I feel strongly that war is not only obscene, it is the ultimate debasement of humankind: war occurs because we have failed. Obscene language, on a much different level to be sure, also results from the user's lazy descent into the banal, doing nothing to elevate either speaker or listener. Do soldiers curse? Of course they do, some of them. I did. I concluded, however, that the reader need not be assaulted with words that add nothing to character insight, plot development, or theme. Instead, I applied "The Aunt Peg Rule": Is it necessary?[1]

During this and other projects, I have found that serendipity plays a part in the creative process. For whatever reason, while researching or at least thinking seriously about a subject, my antennae seem to home in on what might otherwise be

---

[1] Aunt Peg is my godmother. Two of her brothers, Dan and Charlie, my father, served overseas during WWII. A nurse, Aunt Peg met her husband Al while he was hospitalized for his wounds.

construed as random conversations, news articles, television shows, or anything that touches, even ever so lightly, on the subject. Sometimes the connections are more direct.

During the very early stages of drafting *Jenny 4*, I happened to be playing golf with a friend and former colleague, Paul Stevens. Since I wasn't quite sure where the idea would ultimately take me at the time, I only offered, "Oh, fiction, this time," when he asked if I was working on another book. He didn't press, but his next comment was curiously helpful, if not quite serendipitous. He recalled a quote a high school teacher made about fiction (original source unknown). "Fiction," Paul remembered, "is the art of telling the truth without having to worry about the facts." That is in fact what I intended from the beginning. I hope I have succeeded.

For the cover photo I have my former company commander and now lifelong friend Michael T. Ruane to thank. The picture shows Mike on the left with his radio-telephone operator, Greg Kitchen, resting during a road security mission somewhere near Dan Tieng, Vietnam.

Ryan Feasel designed the cover. Thank you, Ryan.

And finally there is Cathy Purdy at BookMasters, Inc. whose patience and guidance helped produce a quality product. Thank you, Cathy.

Chapter 1

August 1966: In the Beginning

> "I never expect a soldier to think."
> *The Devil's Disciple*, Act II
> George Bernard Shaw

He is the most fascinating man I ever met, perhaps the most fascinating man who ever lived. You decide. I'll present the truth as I know it and, then, you decide. Amidst the natural beauty of war-scarred Vietnam I witnessed in him acts of human dignity, personal sacrifice, and selfless kindness. Without being maudlin about it, I saw him live, truly live, those hoary traditions of faith, hope, and charity—preached generously, practiced miserly. More, though, he inspired the same in all whom he touched, as well as all who had heard about and sought to be touched by him. A man of action without bravado; a man capable of long, deep thought who did not, could not abandon the world or the people who suffered in it; a compassionate human being. Have I missed anything?

Yes, humility. Above all, he was a humble man. And there is one more thing about him I could not have known during our time together. He had suffered. By the simplest of definitions, war provokes suffering: physical pain, emotional torment. Some get over it to an extent, that is, they get on with their lives after the immediacy of war passes. Some are scarred for the rest of their lives. Some rise above it.

I wonder what it is about war that brings out the worst in some, the best in others. How can members of the same species act so profoundly different toward each other? Some turn downright nasty. Others, despite the cruelty they witness on a grand scale, numbed by the numbers alone of incidental atrocities and random victims, shield themselves within a cocoon of seeming indifference to the horrific acts they cannot deny. I know how perfunctory it sounds to reduce the complexities of war to a simplistic statement about the presence of good and evil in the world. For it would be more than presumptuous to claim that I, Nick Calloway from Harrison, New Jersey, could decide, or claim, or even surmise that that man over there is inherently bad. That one, too. But he, he is good, and he, and she.

In general, I cannot do that; nor, I feel comfortable in saying, can anyone. Then along comes the exception that proves the rule, one who rises above the banal. He stands out immediately because he is so unlike so many of us. He travels through life, unlike ourselves, without the baggage of pettiness and jealousy. He is a man obviously at peace with himself, not oblivious to events and circumstances, but also not allowing them to influence or control him in any way. Fortunate indeed the person who knows this man. More fortunate the person who shares time and space and experiences with him, who learns from him. Most fortunate the person who lives on to tell this man's story. Call me lucky, I guess.

Before I begin, however, I need to relate the circumstances that led to my meeting him, how I got to know and learn from him, how I lived on to tell his story. I didn't always feel so lucky, you see, certainly not that steamy August afternoon in 1966 when I sat at the kitchen table to open the mail after work. "Greetings." I needed to read no further to know that my Uncle Sam wanted me to leave a decent union job at the ball bearing factory, check in with my draft board, take a physical, and step forward with raised right hand while swearing to uphold something or other of the United States of America. You're (about to be) in the Army, boy. Lucky me, I guess.

I could have tried to avoid The Draft as so many nineteen-year-olds were doing. I had spent one year in college, didn't like it, and left. Okay, let's see, I could have my 2-S (student) deferment reinstated by quitting my pretty well-paying job and enrolling in another school, not to become an accountant or a doctor—ha, ha—but only to maintain my status as civilian. I'm not so smart, but I wasn't so dumb that I couldn't see that return to academia for me at the time represented an escape not a pursuit. I had superficial feelings about the war in Vietnam neither supporting it or detesting it so much that I wanted to run around a campus carrying a "Hey, Hey, LBJ, How Many Kids Did You Kill Today?" sign. Anyway, I took the return to college option off the table right away.

The other path to perpetual civilianhood guys were taking was the 4-F route. I was a decent athlete in my day—Oh, God, was I so old that "my day" had passed forever? —so I didn't see that as a viable out. No Clark Kent, you understand, but I was still a pretty decent specimen of post-adolescent maleness, even if I had already begun thinking of athletic accomplishments as part of my glorious, never to be repeated past. I was too vain to have anyone, much less a faceless draft board, label me unfit for anything.

The short of it is that I got drafted. There would be a physical, but for me that was a formality. Almost a joke. But nearly half the guys who boarded the school bus taking us to the induction center in Newark were carrying manila envelopes stuffed with medical records of all types they hoped would get them declared 4-F. And for some the ruse worked. I've said that the physical was "almost" a joke, and it was; the attempts to dodge the draft for medical reasons were not. There were claims of asthma and things like that. What turned out to be the most successful—in terms of convincing—evidence, however, were the x-rays guys brought attesting to their hernias. Those guys were among the most physically fit. They were serious body builders, almost all former high school lettermen. They were sent home on a bus while I and hundreds of others went to Fort Dix. And the rest, as is said, is history.

Summer Heat

August in New Jersey. Hot! Hot? I would soon discover what it really meant to be hot, Southeast Asian style. Summer all year long. My government had issued me a non-deniable invitation to stop whatever it was I was doing with my life at the time and join ranks with many of my generation who had not wrangled some sort of deferment. The escalation in numbers of American troops destined for duty in South Vietnam had begun under President Lyndon B. Johnson and his band of advisers led by Whiz Kid Secretary of Defense, Robert S. McNamara, whom he had inherited from his assassinated predecessor, John F. Kennedy. Lucky me, oh lucky me; I got caught in that draft.

Caught in a whirlwind is more like it. Swoosh, just like that, I'm in the Army . . . kind of. I'm on a bus filled with a bunch of other lucky guys—we're in the Army because we passed a perfunctory physical exam in Newark, but we're still dressed in our civvies—and we're headed for the reception center at Fort Dix in central New Jersey about 60 miles away. In and out of Dix in three days was the scuttlebutt, which is actually Navy talk but didn't make any difference to us soldiers-to-be dressed in jeans (we called them dungarees in those days) or shorts and tee shirts. Some guy in the back of the bus blurted out to no one in particular that his cousin Freddie "got drafted six months ago, spent three days at Dix, went somewhere down south for training, and was right now getting his butt shot at in the boonies over in Nam."

Reception?

"Move it, move it, move it. Let's go, let's go. Off that bus and line up over there. Move it, move it, move it. Get the lead out. I ain't got no patience for no slackers in This Man's Army."

What man, I'm thinking. Which man? Who's The Man? Is he The Man? For a guy with his own army I'm thinking he could use a refresher course in the English language; I'm thinking this, but I'm not saying it out loud.

"Hey, you."

"Me?"

"Yeah, you. Move it."

"Yes, sir." I swallowed the pride, latent until that precise moment, of actually having spent one year in college. Pointing out this angry man's grammatical deficiencies could be of no possible benefit to my immediate situation.

"Who you callin' sir?" he screams in my face with crooked veins popping out of his temples and long, straight ones bulging from both sides of his neck. "You see these stripes on my arm, boy?" He didn't wait for an answer. "I work for a living, son. You will call me Sergeant. Understand?"

"Yes sir, Sergeant."

"Ah, get in that formation and shutchyer mouth. Move it, move it, move it."

Hup, two, three, four. Next thing you know the whole busload of us are standing single file in our colorful, dare I say stylish, array of civilian underwear in a hollow, high ceiling building. Once to the head of the line, which took about an hour to get to, in less than ten minutes I'm carrying everything I will wear for the foreseeable future in that man's army: boots and shoes—low quarters, they called them—green calf-length socks, green boxers and tee shirts, jungle fatigues, baseball cap, and khaki pants with matching poplin shirts. "Poplin?" I mumble to no one in particular. The guy standing in his skivvies behind me, laden with an identical load of Government Issue duds in his arms, says with a roll of his eyes, a smirk on his lips, and in an almost bored tone of assumed authority, "Don't bother asking." It was Freddie in Nam's cousin from the back of the bus. How come this guy knows so much about the Army?

Upon reaching the last station a soldier about my age in a sweat-stained green tee shirt passes a duffel bag to another soldier our age in matching sweat-stained green tee shirt. The second soldier glances at my paperwork, prepares a stencil, and spray paints my name and serial number on the long canvas bag. I didn't know I had a serial number. Guess I really am in the Army. I'm a real soldier. Freddie's cousin, too; and now I know from his stenciled duffel bag that his name is Cox.

"Got a first name, Cox?"
"Adam. You're, uh, Calloway."
"Nick."

Hup, two, three, four. Double time march. Eight, ten, twelve blocks later Sir Sergeant halts the puffing lot of us in front of a two-story wooden building that looks exactly like every other two-story buff with brown trim wooden building within eyeshot. "When I give the order for the sorry lot of youze to fall out," he screams not quite as violently as he had at the bus, "youze will hustle into this here barracks, place your duffel bags at the foot of the first bunk you come to, take care of business in the latrine if youze have to, and fall back out here in formation. Youze have ten minutes starting one minute ago. Fall out!"

Hup, two, three, four. Double time march. We're standing in line again, having already learned our first Army motto:

Hurry up and wait! This time we get to keep our clothes on, from the waist down at least. Holding baseball cap, fatigue shirt, and green tee shirt, we shuffle slowly through a gauntlet of ghouls in white lab coats. One or two inject single needles into a shoulder, one or two press guns loaded with multiple needles charged with who knows what into the other. The shots didn't hurt that much. Well, they didn't hurt me that much. I suppose the two guys passed out on cots behind a white-curtained room divider on wheels might disagree. An early-twenty-something soldier in fatigues sitting at a small table at the end of the line—later identified as a medic by Adam Cox, the self-proclaimed and by now recognized default expert on all things military ever since the bus trip out of downtown Newark—gave each of us a card about the size of a driver's license and said, "Stick this in your wallet and don't lose it or we'll have to do this all over again."

I looked at the card. Plague? I had just been inoculated against, among other medieval blights that wiped out legions of Europeans, plague. Except for the dull soreness in my shoulders and the slight heaviness I felt running down the insides of my biceps, the shots hadn't bothered me. But where on God's earth—or in This Man's Army for that matter—would I, would we, be exposed to plague?

God, are you listening? Get me out of here. Please.

Sir Sergeant stood outside the rear door to greet each of us personally upon exit. "Feel all right, boy?" he asked one at a time with a momentary, albeit unconvincing, air of caring. "Good. Now put them shirts back on. You ain't at some beach somewheres down the Jersey shore. You're in This Man's Army, boys." As our amorphous group began to gain mass outside what I guess was some sort of medical building, Sarge—this seemed an acceptable moniker of compromise between him and us regarding his name and rank—allowed that we could "smoke 'em if you got 'em." I wasn't a smoker yet, but I started to wonder about the relative merits of dying from heart disease or lung cancer before the plague got me.

About nine-thirty that first night in This Man's Army Sarge barges into the barracks. "Listen up, everybody," he says louder than necessary. "I'm gonna walk up one side of this sorriest excuse for quarters I ever seen in twenty-three years in This Man's Army and down the other. If I touch the foot rail of your bunk, you will immediately tie a towel around it." Naturally, he touches mine . . . Cox's too. Having now returned to his original rostrum near the entry to our home away from home, he explains: "Youze guys with the towels lucked out. Youze have KP in the morning. Lights out."

Okay, I think to myself. So what? It's not like I had anything else pressing on my calendar. But what's with the towels? Silly boy, Lucky, you'll find out soon enough. Don't let it worry you. Get some sleep.

At three-thirty in the morning a goon with a flashlight traipses into the barracks and bangs an aluminum baton on the foot rail of every bunk with a towel wrapped around it, caring not a whit that he actually prodded the entire barracks into a groaning herd. "Let's go. All you Kitchen Police take care of your business and be lined up outside in a column of twos in twenty minutes." As my reluctant body followed my still sleeping feet to the floor, I noticed Cox adjust his entire body under his blanket into a near fetal position more suitable to prolonging his sleep.

"What the . . ." The towel he had obediently draped on the foot rail for Sir Sergeant last night was gone. He grinned at me, winked, and whispered, "Who's gonna know?" How can I not love this guy? "And by the way, Nicky, I like my eggs over easy and my bacon crisp." Grrr! How can I not hate this guy? Nobody except family calls me Nicky.

Private Goon didn't bother with the hup, two, three, fours. We just kind of fell two-by-two into a cockeyed line and followed this company "runner," who, it turns out, had pulled this overnight duty, just as we had pulled KP, and was no more pleased than we to be roaming the litter free streets of Fort Dix in the middle of the night.

A Search for Military Intelligence

In between scrubbing pots and pans inside the mess hall and garbage cans out back of it during this, our first real day on the job, we kitchen policemen got to double time march to yet another two-story wooden building that looked exactly like that sorry excuse for quarters we had laid us down to sleep in so few hours ago and the torture chamber where the white coats swore, "This won't hurt a bit." Only this two-story wooden building had school desks and proctors who acted more like hall monitors than teachers.

"Sit down. Eyes on your own paper," et cetera, et cetera, et cetera. Funny, I thought, This Man's Army's reception center tests us after it admits us. I'm wondering if anyone flunks out, I mean, after having a serial number stenciled on a duffel bag and all that. Could I have developed a hernia from all that duffel lugging?

Well, anyway, I must have passed the tests, even though policing the kitchen starting at 0400—Armyspeak for Godawful early—and double time marching to and fro had knocked me out of my best test taking frame of mind. There was this one guy, though, named Forest who to my knowledge never finished the tests. Every time the sergeant in charge called "Time," he'd jump right into Forest's face and say something like, "Didn't finish that one either, eh, boy?" There was no way to tell if Forest was trying to flunk out of the Army or whether he was just no good at taking tests. When the ordeal ended—for the rest of us—the three-striper ordered Forest to stay. We found out later from him in the barracks that the sergeant made him take the entire battery of tests three times. "I never did finish even one of 'em," Forest whined. And we knew from the tone of his tinny voice that he wasn't faking bad test taking to get out of the Army. We also figured that Forest would be gone the next day. Why give us all these tests, the argument went, if they don't do something with you if you fail them? Cox commented to himself with a hint of scorn, "Dang! Why didn't I think of that?"

Forest stayed. Lucky him. Lucky us, we all passed the ex post facto entrance exam.

On the third day at Fort Dix Sir Sergeant roused us from the dead of a deep, deep sleep to the familiar rumble of, "move it, move it, move it." None of us had pulled KP that day, that pleasure having been delegated to the recruit class that arrived the day after our own reception, now missing out on a full night's sleep in the barracks next door. Instead, we hurried up and waited outside the mess hall, ate a surprisingly decent breakfast of "take all you want but eat all you take," and hup, two, three, foured for the last time to our barracks at Fort Dix, which by the way I could never have found in a month of Sundays if I had to do it alone, day or night.

Hup, two, three, four. Hup, two, three, four. Hup, two, three, four. No double time march this time. Just a subdued "move it" every now and then to keep us mindful that, lest we dare forget, we were still in That Man's Army. We arrived at a parking lot at which commercial buses sat waiting for us with diesels running. The buses transported us to a train that transported us to a land far, far away.

Like Pigs in a Polk

"Move it, move it, y'all, move it," barked a clone of Sir Sergeant from Fort Dix who let it be known that he personally commanded "Thish Man'sh Army" at our new home away from home. "Yoush are now in Thish Man'sh Army, Fawt Poke, Looshianna." How many army's we got, I thought, not recognizing my own insidious descent into Armyspeak, while trying with no success to ignore the spittle spray spewing from his buck toothed overbite.

In a relatively short time—two months of basic infantry training and two more of advanced infantry training—I actually looked and felt like a soldier—a misherable, shorry excushe for a sholdier," to be sure, as Sir Sergeant and his complicit drill instructors were quick and happy to remark without conscious or intended provocation on our part—but a soldier nonetheless. By training's end at Fort Polk, I had earned a Private First Class stripe to sew on my sleeve, an Expert Marksman badge certifying my proficiency with the M-16 rifle, and a blue shoulder cord and dickey to be worn with dress uniforms, signifying that I was part of the proudest and longest standing of all traditions in the citizen soldier-swelled ranks of the United States Army. Within the combat arms I was an "ultimate weapon," an infantryman. I was a full fledged grunt. And I was proud.

We all felt proud of ourselves after the graduation ceremony on the parade grounds, even Forest. I remember how tall he stood and we, his squadmates, felt real pride for him, too. We had all endured the breakdown before the buildup. The drill instructors yelled and cussed and did everything in their autocratic power to make us feel miserable and useless, while all the while teaching us combat survival skills—although "teaching" is a word I use here only for convenience, you understand. Once we realized that we could endure whatever misery they subjected us to, we started to come together like a team—not a football team or a basketball team or a baseball team, mind you—a team of honest to goodness soldiers. We helped each other ford streams, climb and descend rocky hills. Heck, we even split up the work load on Friday nights to get ready for Saturday morning inspections. McDonald spit-shined every low quarter and boot in the squad. Bonds and Fauvre scoured the bathroom. Fisher mopped and polished the tiled floor in the squad bay and all the way down the hall. I was the Friday night ironer; every guy in the squad bought a can of spray starch at the PX and gave it to me with his pile of wrinkled pants and shirts.

Here's a little trick I mastered after the first inspection at Fort Polk. (Okay, okay, I'll admit it, Cox engineered the scheme. Anyway . . .) Whoever was doing the inspecting, usually the company commander, a captain—but sometimes the platoon leader, a lieutenant—would generally open one or two lockers at random to see that everything was stowed properly. In the case of the shirts, the left sleeves all had to face the same way and line up in a continuous, equidistant overlap. The inspector never, and I mean never, looked past the starched stiff sleeves if they were aligned properly. So, living up to the reputation of the resourceful American soldi (Bless you, Private Cox!), on Friday nights I cut my ironing load in half just by ironing the daylights out of one side and one sleeve per shirt. Let me tell you, those sleeves had so much starch in them that four of them could have anchored a pup tent in a hurricane.

The Army has a name for this activity that takes place in a barracks the night before an inspection. They call it a GI party. Derivation unknown, but nonetheless a typical Army distortion of conventional English usage. There's no doubt in my military mind (an expression I picked up from Fort Polk's Sir Sergeant who owned that particular subsidiary of Thish Man'sh Army) that Friday night fraternity parties we knew were going on all across collegiate America had nothing in common with our mopping, slopping, rubbing, scrubbing affairs. We also knew, however, without ever admitting it to each other, that a bond was forming. This included barely trainable Forest and Cox, the perpetual rebel. "They can cut my hair and make me wear silly clothes," Cox declared one night. "They can give me a gun and make me sleep on the ground. But they ain't gonna make me something I ain't." Forest nodded, giving his unequivocal and unsolicited agreement, lacking the social and verbal skills to express himself with Cox's eloquence.

Nobody blamed Forest that Saturday morning when Captain Whatever His Name Was decided to open his locker during what was, to that point, a routine inspection. We all stood at attention at the foot of our bunks while the captain looked at whatever he felt like looking at in the room or on our persons, asking random questions. What's the chamber pressure of the M-16 rifle, MacDonald?" he asked gruffly while checking Fisher's bunk. "Sir, the chamber pressure of the M-16 rifle is fifty thousand pounds per square inch, Sir."

I stood in the row opposite Forest, two bunks to the left, next to the window. When Captain Whatever approached his locker, I inhaled very deeply and caught sight of Cox rolling his eyes like he had a premonition. Clink, clank, open. I sighed inwardly in relief—feeling quite proud of myself, actually—when I saw those sleeves standing tall, the crease sharp enough to slice a tomato. The captain lingered to admire the ironing job, I logically thought to myself. His head rose so he could gaze upon the shelf above the clothes pole. Oh, no, Forest, I can see the box of laundry detergent from here. That's supposed to be in your foot locker. Cox closed his eyes tight and his whole face wrinkled.

"What's this, Private Forest?"

"Sir?"

"This . . ." the captain said as he reached for the offending carton. Can't tell what actually happened next, it happened so fast, but as the training company commander reached toward the box of Tide it fell forward and spilled its scented contents down his shirt and created a beady, dry puddle around his glassy-toed jump boots. He stepped back in silence and stood facing the locker for about ten seconds that seemed like an hour. Cox opened one eye. The captain turned, ignored Forest, and walked smartly out the door of the squad bay. Ten minutes or so later, Sir Sergeant returned to inform us that all leaves were canceled for the weekend. The squad was placed on barracks restriction. We failed the inspection and there was no make-up.

Group anger settled in quickly. Funny, though, we were mad at the Army, specifically its non-elected leaders, not at Forest. We kind of rallied around him like we would a little brother who is about to suffer Mom's wrath for something he couldn't help doing, like spilling his lima beans on the kitchen floor. He really couldn't help it, you know, squaring his locker away, and we knew that. Just like when we went to the firing range the first time.

The lead instructor, a no nonsense sergeant first class, saw something right away in Forest that caused him to walk briskly to his firing position and snatch the rifle right out of his hands. "Give me that piece, Soldier. Sergeant Thomas, remove this man from my rifle range." After that, Forest was never allowed to be on the firing line with the squad. He had to remove the camouflage cover from his steel pot, instantly identifying him as "different," someone to be avoided and not trusted. The entire cadre on the range referred to Forest for the rest of training as a dud. (Some lifers apparently had their own army—we knew two of them personally. Cox pointed out that this guy only had a rifle range. Who's the real dud here, Sarge?)

We couldn't do anything about the Army's insistence on dressing Forest up like a soldier. But even when his inspection screw up cost us the loss of weekend privileges, we didn't blame him. We blamed the Army. The Army drafted him and then kept him even though, we all knew, he couldn't pass the tests they gave him after they issued him a serial numbered duffel bag and filled it with brand new clothes. Then they called him a dud. "They" called him a dud, but "we" never did.

Eight weeks of harassment culminated with a surprisingly stately graduation. At the end of the ceremony we all threw our class A hats in the air like they do at West Point. We weren't cadets, we didn't just receive a college degree, and we were only privates first class, not officers and gentlemen. All the same, we graduated, all of us, including Forest. They didn't break him, and they didn't break us. I believe that it was in spite of them and their sometimes cruel training methods, not because of them, that we came to care so deeply for each other.

Even though Forest was basically a loner—no buddies from the same town or anything like that—he was one of us from the start: a draftee, just like most of us. Some nights I lay in my bunk thinking about an incident involving Forest during the day, he getting chewed out for some silly reason or another and none of us being able to speak up or defend him in any way. I knew it was wrong of me to think in these terms but I'd still think, hey, if they can do it to him, "the least of my brethren," they can do it to me. That kind of thinking led me to thoughts like, what am I doing here? It was a reasonable guess that the whole sorry lot of us would end up in Vietnam. In some esoteric way never ever explained to us during all our training we were about to be called upon to serve our country and defend (proselytize?) the American way of life, whatever that is.

Sure I love my country. Sure I think it's important for us Americans to help other people be free. But I sure don't like having a succession of chronically grumpy career soldiers scream in my face for no reason at all that I am worthless, that they will tell me when I can sit, stand, walk, eat. And I sure don't like the treatment Forest went through. This is not the America I love.

Chapter 2

October 1966: Mail Call

"Sir, more than kisses, letters mingle souls."
Letters to Severall Personages, "To Sir Henry Wotton"
John Donne

Mrs. Calloway
305 Ann Street
Harrison, NJ

              PFC Nicholas Calloway
              "A" Company, 3/21
              96th LIB, APO San Francisco

[Note to Reader: I didn't collect stamps or coins or pursue any sedentary hobbies as a kid. I didn't stash virtually untouched baseball cards in my socks and underwear drawer. Some of my friends traded cards with each other trying to amass a complete set of Yankees or Dodgers or Giants. Maybe you did, too. A few guys went for oddball collections, like the Mickey Mantle-Duke Snyder-Willie Mays combination, which led to never ending, passionate playground arguments about who the best center fielder in New York was; make that "in the world." That and similar curiously serious debates about players and games and teams followed them into adulthood. I never understood any of that. Still don't.

Whenever I picked up my packet of Topp's at Joe's Candy Store—he called it a confectionery emporium—I was chomping on the huge rectangle of stale bubble gum before I got out the door. I would then put those cards to their best possible use, lacing them, all stiff and shiny, through the spokes of my J.C. Higgins which created an illusion of speed when the bike was in motion; even better than that, they caused an uninterrupted clacking sound that annoyed most adults in the neighborhood as the cards slapped against the fender's edge.

So I'm not sure why I kept all those letters from home when I was in the Army. I'm not a keeper. Just as puzzling to me is why family and friends kept letters from us. Thank God they did, for those letters have helped me piece together this story. Now I offer them to you in the same spirit I believe they were written. On one level they merely chronicle activities in people's lives during a particular point in time, something like the episodes Huck told us about, like the time he and Jim—spokesmen for the illiterati of their day—rafted down the Mississippi River. More important, however, is the depth of raw emotion apparent to me reading them years later. Every one was a love letter. Well, maybe not "every" one.

Letter writers expose themselves willingly and quite thoroughly. "This is what is in my heart," the personal letter says. "I want to share it with you." When we place one letter, or episode, near another and then another, the montage forces us to look past the who, what, and wheres of the Huck and Jim in us. Rather, we begin to discover that which is at the core of our relationships, the humanity beneath our humanness.

The story you have begun to read, the one I have begun to write, might not have become much more than a collection of anecdotes about a city kid who finds himself in the middle of a war in the middle of a jungle. The letters, though, the letters written by me and to me as well as those that others so

graciously allowed me to share with you on these pages, broadened the definition of my life. The farther I traveled, you see, the more I craved knowledge of where I came from. The letters, my precious letters, weren't "from" home, they "were" home.
   And so I share them with you.]
   Here's the first.

   Dear Nicky,
   I know it must be hard for you to write very often but Daddy and I miss you and feel helpless not knowing what you're doing or where you're going. Well, mostly it's me that feels that way. Daddy doesn't like to talk much about you being in the army, what with that war going on over there in Vietnam. He sits in his Lay-Z-Boy after supper and reads the paper just like always. He keeps reading when the news comes on, but I know he's listening harder when Walter Cronkite starts talking about you boys in uniform. He said just the other day that the president was about to send a whole bunch more over there, said it had something to do with the Gulf of Tonkin. I didn't have no idea where this gulf was but Daddy said he did. Anyway, Nicky, please write to us whenever you can. I pray for you every day. Happy Halloween.

All my love,
Mom

Chapter 3

December 1966: Fire in the Hole

> "On, ye brave,
> Who rush to glory, or the grave!"
> Thomas Campbell

"Spread out. Everybody down. Stay down. Squad leaders over here on the double." I couldn't tell where these orders were coming from or who was giving them. I had been in country less than two weeks and now found myself on my first combat patrol, a platoon size operation that began a short helicopter hop from our base camp at Chu Lai, I Corps, in the northeast quadrant of South Vietnam, somewhere near the South China Sea. I had been assigned to—it took me a long time to get this right—Alpha Team, Second Squad, Second Platoon, Alpha Company, Third Battalion, Twenty-first Infantry, One Hundred and Ninety-sixth Light Infantry Brigade (mailing address: PFC Nicholas Calloway, "A," 3/21, 196th LIB, APO San Francisco). The choppers had dropped us into a small clearing and I'm not exactly sure how this happened but we ended up on our bellies in a relatively straight line across about five or ten meters inside a wood line. (Although Americans reckon distance in yards and miles, the United States Army standard is meters and kilometers, clicks—one of many Armyisms I never figured out.) Second squad was in the middle with first to our right and third to our left.

"Sergeant Smith, take your squad and proceed straight ahead until you reach a clearing," Lieutenant Troy ordered. "That should be about two hundred and fifty to three hundred meters due west according to this sorry excuse for a map. Fire a single shot into the air when you get there, wait five seconds, then fire two more. Jones, Murfee, spread your men forward for flank security north and south, keep a man looking rearward, then stay put until Smith signals all clear."

"Yes, sir."

Perceptions of This Man's Army changed for me almost literally in an instant. Even though Sir Sergeant at Dix and his twin brother from another mother at Polk had conditioned an immediate hustle response with their "move it, move it, move its," the much younger Sergeant Smith's use of those words carried an infinitely greater sense of urgency. "When I give the word," he said with relative calmness, I thought, given present circumstances, "Alpha fan out to the left, Bravo to the right. Then we're going to leap frog ten meters at a time, Alpha first. Got it," he asked rhetorically. "All right now, everybody, move it."

Advancing an infantry squad one fire team at a time allows one team to lay down a base of fire if the enemy is present, effectively—hopefully—keeping his head down and nullifying incoming heat while the other team moves forward. The teams alternate the tactic until they reach the objective and knock out the enemy or force him to retreat. Standard Operating Procedure. Sure, I had thought to myself back at Polk when this particular SOP was explained to the sorry lot of us sitting like kindergartners at story time and then practiced again and again on the drill field. Sure, just like that, we'll play checkers with the enemy all the way to his king row, knock him off his throne or out of his bunker or whatever, and chalk it all up to SOP. God, This Man's Army is good. I remember wanting to ask the youngish second lieutenant in charge if GIs followed this particular SOP at Normandy Beach on D-Day. But I digress.

Let me tell you, nobody spouting SOPs in any man's Army stateside mentioned the pucker factor which roughly translates to a sudden, involuntary tightening of the body's major muscle groups, including and especially the gluteus maximus, the butt. Thus, the "pucker." What happens is that in the face of real or even imagined peril the body excites itself into a kind of high. Sweat appears, of course, accompanied by this amazing sensation of alertness. Adrenaline, maybe. Most likely. You react intuitively, almost animalistically, to the slightest sounds and flashes of movement, trying actually not to overreact, all the while your butt cheeks are puckered so that you walk kind of funny. The body would likely incinerate itself, I think, if it ran very long in this aroused state, because the heart is also pounding, pounding, pounding heavily against sopping shirts. Anyway, right now in this my first action in the war zone, armed with live bullets and hand grenades, my body was definitely running in pucker mode.

"Alpha, go," Sergeant Smith yelled. We went. We dropped. No enemy fire. "Bravo, go." They did. They passed us. They dropped. No fire. We did this three or four times. "Alpha, up on line with Bravo, no farther, and down. Okay, listen up, everybody. Doesn't look like Charley's out there. Everyone on your feet, stay on line, and we'll keep going 'till we see the break. Eddie, get your compass out and keep us dead west."

"You got it."

"On your feet," Sergeant Smith yelled left and right, resembling a quarterback audibilizing at the line of scrimmage. "Move out. Don't bunch up. No hurry. And stay on line."

The pucker eased but the sweat kept pouring as I tried to focus on everything: the bushes and trees, looking for snipers; the ground, looking for booby traps and the punji pits they warned us about at Polk; the other guys in the squad, looking for signs of what I should do next; and the sky, looking for divine guidance to get me through this day, this test, this moment. We advanced slowly, cautiously, through what turned out to be more woods than jungle. I marveled at how professional my newfound comrades appeared in their movements, wondering all the while—worrying, really—if they sensed my fear. Sweat poured down my brow, down my neck, down the small of my back, trickling into the pucker zone; it soaked my fatigues; even my feet felt squishy. I gripped my rifle as firmly as I had ever gripped a baseball bat and swung it randomly in broad, rapid sweeps.

"Hey, man," Tommy to my right says. "Keep that piece in front of you. What do you want to do, put a hole through me or something?"

"Oh, yeah. Yeah. Sorry. Sorry 'bout that."

A couple days later, having returned to base camp, we—Tommy and I—were sitting on our cots emptying bullets from magazines and wiping every one to prevent any trace of corrosion that would cause a shell to jam the M-16 rifle. I needed to talk about what happened out there.

"Yeah," he said matter of factly, "I was scared, too. We're all scared. That's what keeps us alive. Fear." He lingered on the word. "Fear," he repeated. "But I ain't scared of dying myself, mind you—don't get me wrong, I don't want to die—nah, I'm scared of you dying because of me not doing my job. That's what scares me. A week ago I never heard of you, didn't know you from the man in the moon. Next thing I know some stranger's sleeping in the cot next to mine. That'd be you. Today, we're brothers. Nick Calloway went through the same hell as Tommy Hajj out there. From now on my job is to see you get back to the real world in one healthy piece. Your job is to buy me a beer when we get there."

"But I was really scared. Puckered," I confessed, appreciating Tommy trying to put me at ease but anxious to unburden myself on him, my new brother, to tell him the whole truth. "When we got to where we could see that clearing, I started to relax. When Sergeant Smith fired the shots to bring up the rest of the platoon, I felt really good, like I . . . like we . . . had accomplished something, even if I didn't know what the heck it was we had accomplished. But when Charley opened fire from the other side of that clearing I froze." Actually, I couldn't remember what happened, I just figured I froze. And by talking the scene out with Tommy I was trying to recreate it.

"You didn't freeze," he said. "You dropped to your gut and returned fire right away, just like you're supposed to."

"I did?"

"You did. Of course you didn't hit anything except worms about ten meters in front of us and tree tops on the other side. But you didn't shoot none of us and you helped keep their heads down for a while. Don't worry about it, you did fine . . . for the first time." Tommy couldn't resist the little dig.

"Thanks. I wish I believed you."

As much as I couldn't remember exactly how I responded to my first act of war—shooting with intent to kill, not to mention being shot at and the possibility of getting killed—nor could I force the first sight of combat death out of my head. Here's what happened.

After Sergeant Smith fired his signal rounds, Lieutenant Troy, the medic, and the radio operator meandered toward us in no particular formation between the first and third squads. Smith had ordered us to spread out three to five meters apart and to keep our eyes on the woodline at the far side of the clearing. In a very short time the first and third squads took up positions on our flanks forming a "U" which effectively provided security north and south so the platoon could proceed with the mission—whatever the mission was. Truth be told, I never actually figured out what the mission was.

Lieutenant Troy made his way toward us at the front line to formulate, I guess, what I recalled Sir Sergeant at Polk had called a "hashty eshtimate of the shityewashion." (That guy really had a funny way with words. And the funniest thing is that I remember every one of them.) Huddled behind a tree trunk with Sergeant Smith, the two strategized over Troy's map which he had spread on the ground. "Radio," Troy yelled, and the operator moved quickly toward the conference. "We'll send the first squad across single file on the north side," I heard Troy say. "Then . . ."

Then, pop, pop, pop from the woods to the front. Then, rat-a-tat-tat from behind. An enemy sniper somehow slipped into the wake of the first and third squads and opened fire with an automatic weapon immediately after a few of his buddies fired single shots at us from the other side. "Ambush." There was yelling and screaming all over the place. If I was scared before, I was near panic now. I turned toward the gunfire to the rear just in time to see the radio operator's steel pot fly off his head . . . what was left of his head. In one continuous, fluid motion his arms flapped out to either side like he was in the middle of a jumping jack and his body jerked forward and he landed face down in the dirt. The PRC-25 strapped to his back rode up to his neck and the handset lay in a pool of his puddling blood. He died instantly. Silently. "Oh, God," I screamed in horror.

"Tommy, I froze. I couldn't move. I wanted to run to him, but I couldn't move."

"It wouldn't have done him no good."

"But I couldn't move. Then more bullets start zinging in from the other direction, from across the clearing we thought was safe. Correction: from across the clearing I thought was safe."

Tommy told me I did the right thing. "You turned toward that woodline and returned fire. It ain't easy to hit something you can't see," he said as consolation. "The whole second squad returned fire, and Charley got his tail out of there. That's what we do when we get snookered into an ambush. That's what you did." He told me MacDuffy in the third squad took out the sniper.

"What was his name," I asked.

"Who?"

"The radio operator. What was his name?"

"Jenny 4. That was his call sign. He told everybody that's what he wanted to be called, Jenny 4. So that's what we called him."

I couldn't live with that. He had a name, a real name, not some Army alias. I had to know his name. I pushed. "What was his name?"

"Lambert. Jake Lambert." Tommy seemed perturbed. "Ah, it don't matter."

I knew Tommy did not want me to press the matter for whatever reason and so I went about wiping my bullets in silence. As I started reloading the first magazine, Tommy reached over and grabbed my wrist. "Man," he said through a scrunched up face, "they don't teach you guys nothing before they send you over here."

"What?"

He slipped the handful of bullets out of the magazine I was loading and proceeded to take the magazine apart: two interlocking sides and a spring, not exactly Space Age technology. "This here's important," he said, now wiping the spring. "If the spring don't work, the ammo don't rise right, and your piece don't work." His eyes stayed fixed on the spring as he continued to wipe it with his rag. "You wipe the spring and the insides of the magazine like this. Make sure you rub everything real good . . . but don't kink the spring. Then you take a little oil, just a little on the rag, and wipe it on the spring like this.

Take the dry part of the rag and wipe it one last time before you put it all back together."

All of this made sense, of course, even to a transplanted city boy who had never held anything resembling a firearm until about four months or so ago, unless you count the Lone Ranger six shooters Santa Claus gave me on my eighth Christmas. "You got to watch how much oil you leave on the spring."

"Why's that?"

"'Cause, number one, you just want enough to prevent rust, and B, you don't want oil to smear all over the cartridges and drip all over the place. Dirt gets in there and . . ." Tommy raised his head slowly, closed his eyes, and inhaled deeply through his nose. "His name was Jake Lambert. The Man swore us in the same day in Philly. He was from Bethlehem, PA. I'm from Emmaus, about ten miles from there, just outside Allentown." Tommy was taking one of his own magazines apart at this point, I did the same with another of mine. I said nothing. What could I say?

"Lamb was the best," Tommy muttered more to himself than to me. "He hated this place, he hated this war. But he loved everybody and everybody loved him right back."

The word love surprised me. I said nothing.

Tommy's eyes moistened. "Never fired his weapon over here. Not one time. Never."

No Closure

Funny thing about war death, those who witness it are denied the rituals that help mourners get through the most difficult first days of their loss. People who live free don't think much about their soldiers somewhere far away at war. Unless they know one personally, they tend to forget that most soldiers at war, particularly the ones out there on the line doing the bleeding, are barely more than teenagers. And like most young people, thankfully, their only experience with death might have been the passing of a grandparent or elderly aunt. They deal with it. The support group kicks in: family gathers, friends come by the funeral parlor, a member of the clergy says the right things; the funeral director sets an appropriately somber mood with flowers, candles, pictures, and a satin cushioned coffin. The well intentioned eulogist at the funeral alludes to the frailty of human life. "Live each day as though it were your last," he might say. "Death is but a part of life." And people of faith, even fledglings in faith like me, find consolation, maybe even strength, in their belief that "this is not the end."

Up until the moment of Jake Lambert's death that pretty much summed up my own experience. Grandma—on my father's side—died when I was thirteen; Pop is still with us. Mom's parents both passed on while I was a little kid, real little, little enough for my parents to shelter me from what was going on at the time. So I don't remember the circumstances of their deaths or how I felt, if indeed I felt anything at all when they were lost to me. It was different with Grandma, because I knew her. I saw her almost every day. I loved her. God, how I loved her.

She died unexpectedly in her sleep one night. The last time I saw her was two days before, a Saturday afternoon, when she gave me fifty cents for sweeping the staircase that rose to my grandparents' second floor apartment. I wasn't allowed to go to the wake—don't really know why—so the enduring picture I have of her is that smile and wink when she said her last words to me: "Don't spend it all in one place, Nicky." I prayed through the whole funeral for God to hold back my tears so I wouldn't look like a baby in front of everybody, not knowing it was okay to cry, not knowing that manliness has nothing to do with the absence of tears. I remember her kindness, her smile, her faith, her patience. I miss her. God, I miss her. But the rituals of the funeral and the family gathering afterward helped me get through the ordeal. I didn't understand at first why people at the house seemed so happy, some even joking about things that had nothing to do with Grandma.

"Grandma is dead," I screamed silently to myself. "What's wrong with you people?" No one noticed me leave the "party" after the funeral. I sat on the back porch, buried my face in my hands, and cried uncontrollably. I could almost hear the last word Grandma said to me, "Nicky"; it pleased me then, comforts me now.

"Oh, there you are," Aunt Patty said when I came back into the kitchen through the back door. "We were wondering where you were, Nick. Here, have a piece of my soda bread. You always liked my soda bread."

"How's high school, Big Guy," Uncle Pete asked. "Boy, I remember my first year in high school . . ." But again I digress. Sorry.

The war death experience is nothing like that. War death is not a natural progression of the life cycle. The body does not concede to cancer or sclerosis or time. War death results from a hostile act precipitated by human failure. Like anybody's grandma, the dead soldier can never return. But unlike grandma's family who eventually accept her passing, the soldier who witnesses war death is doomed to random recall of the event. He relives the moment of violent death many, many times, for many, many years. For him the sight, sound, and smell of that death create a continuous present from which he cannot escape. That present bears none of death's euphemistic accouterments available to civilized people: no flowers, no psalms, no burial, no celebration of life. Rather, the moment of the body's defilement in combat remains forever present. The final, enduring image of war death is horror.

JENNY 4

Before I knew Jake Lambert's name, I saw shards of his skull pierce the air, I saw his brain burst, I saw his body dappled in his own gore. I never saw his face again. I can't find comfort, like Tommy can to some degree, in fond memories of Jenny 4's goodness. I lost a comrade I never knew somewhere in I Corps that day and the image I bear forever is the bloody inside of the back of his head.

"Medic!"

Lieutenant Troy's call for the medic was a meaningless reflex action.

To tell the truth I have to surmise just about everything that happened after that, everything between Lieutenant Troy's call for the medic on the battlefield and the deferred post mortem conversation with Tommy Hajj in our squad tent in base camp. I can't be sure but I think it went something like this: The shooting stopped. The shouting stopped. The platoon set up a perimeter around the clearing into which someone tossed a smoke grenade, purple smoke I'm pretty sure; I could be wrong. A helicopter swooped down and took Jake Lambert away; it's called a dust off. I have no idea what happened to the VC sniper MacDuffy killed. We walked around the jungle for two days—the woods got thicker and thicker and we needed to keep trading places at the front of the patrol because the point man had to cut a path with a machete. Very hard work. I do remember that part, mostly because the blister in the palm of my right hand wouldn't let me forget. We reached a path that led to a road that brought us to a village where we boarded trucks—deuce-and-a-halfs—that returned us to base camp. I think that's the way it happened. Pretty sure. Can't swear to it.

"And don't jam twenty bullets into the magazine," Tommy said.

"But it holds twenty."

"Yeah. And squeezing twenty bullets into a magazine ruins the spring. Don't jam twenty bullets into the magazine. Seventeen. Eighteen, tops."

"Calloway." It was Sergeant Smith.

"Yeah."

"Troy wants to see me and you over at the mess tent. Right away."

Chapter 4

December 1966: Mail Call

> "From ignorance our comfort flows,
> The only wretched are the wise."
> "To the Honorable Charles Montague"
> Matthew Prior

Mrs. Calloway
305 Ann Street
Harrison, NJ

        PFC Nicholas Calloway
        "A" Company, 3/21
        196th LIB, Fort Polk, Louisiana

Dear Nicky,

Thank you so much for calling from Fort Polk before you left. Daddy was mad he missed the call. Doctor D'Ambola says he ought to cut down on the cigarettes but he's still puffing away. Actually, he seems to be smoking more in the house than he used to, especially after supper. Since you didn't know what your new address would be, I'm going to mail this letter to you at Fort Polk and just hope you get it. We don't understand what this fighting in Vietnam is all about—well I don't, that's for sure. I wish you didn't have to go. Do you remember that summer you went away to camp and I had to sew labels with your name into all your clothes? Oh how you hated that. First you wanted to go, then you didn't want to go. But in the end you had a good time. I knew you would. I was so proud of you when you got on the bus carrying that canvas gym bag Daddy loaned you. That's kind of how I felt the morning you left for Fort Dix. I was real proud. Daddy didn't say much but I know he was real proud too. He forgot about that little argument you had the night before.

    Then you went to Louisiana and now you're headed for Vietnam. I know this sounds awful but I didn't even know where Vietnam was up until Daddy showed me on the globe in your bedroom the other night. I wasn't even sure where Louisiana was. I hope that army knows what a good boy they have going over there to Vietnam. You write and tell us anything you need when you get there, Nicky. I'll send it out right away. I'll keep writing even if I don't hear from you. If that army can get you and all those other boys over to Vietnam, I guess they can get a mother's letter to her son somehow. Stay safe, Nicky. Merry Christmas wherever you are.

                      All my love and prayers,

                      Mom

Mrs. Thelma Johnson
1860 Riverview Drive
New Orleans, Louisiana

                Private Tyrone Derkin
                "A" Company, 3/21
                196th LIB, APO San Francisco

My Ty,

Mammy and I look forward to your letters every week and that last one set us to singing so loud Mrs. Black come running up the stairs. It didn't surprise us none that Uncle Sam got smart and made you a cook over there in Vietnam. I knowed all the time you was following me around the kitchen when you was just toddling you was picking up my recipes. I'm sure you're getting real good at it. It's in your blood. But tell me, son, do you boys have the fixings to bake an apple pie from scratch? I been bragging to Mr. Dellacroix about all that cooking experience you're getting in the army and how I know you'll be ready to hire on in one of them fancy restaurants down on Bourbon Street when you come home. No more washing dishes at Frenchy's Diner for you. He says he's going to talk to some people, says he's going to be your reference. Now about them presents you asked for for Christmas. Don't you worry none. They'll be there if I have to fly over that ocean and bring them to you myself. You just keep looking for that box in the mail and don't go opening it up until Christmas Day. You watch out for yourself, Tyrone. The Lord answered my prayers when he made sure you wasn't doing no fighting over there. That cooking job is the work of God's hand. Praise the Lord. You can thank Him by being the best cook in the whole United States Army. You're already the best grandson any woman could ever have.

> Bless you,
> Grannie

P.S. Your Mom's been working real hard. She told me to tell you she loves you.

Chapter 5

January 1967: New Assignment

> "At the hand of every man's brother
> will I require the life of man."
> Genesis, 9:5

The mess tent doubled as a multipurpose room in base camp between meal times, almost like the day room in our brick barracks back at Polk. Without the television, pool table, stuffed chairs, and vending machines. Well, maybe the company mess tent in my Chu Lai home away from home wasn't much like the day room at Fort Polk after all. But it was nevertheless a place to catch a decent cup of coffee anytime, day or night; and when necessary it became a meeting room.

"Sir, you wanted to see me and Private Calloway?"

"Yes, I do, Sergeant Smith," Lieutenant Troy replied. "Get yourselves a cup of coffee, first, or a cold drink if you like."

"Thank you, Sir. We will."

This was the first time I had ever been invited to have a civil conversation with an officer, or even a noncom, come to think of it. It never happened stateside at Dix or Polk. From out of nowhere that silly line from The Wizard of Oz popped into my head: You're not in Kansas anymore. I knew—at least I thought I knew—that I hadn't screwed up in the short time I had been in Vietnam. I hadn't done anything great yet, either, so this sure as heck wasn't a medal-pinning-on ceremony.

"At ease, fellas. I have something important to say, and it affects both of you. So I want you to understand my decision."

"Sir, would you pass the sugar," Sergeant Smith asked, almost as though he wasn't paying any particular attention to our platoon leader, even though no doubt he was.

As Lieutenant Troy reached for the bowl, I noticed the Ranger patch on his sleeve near his left shoulder, then the paratrooper wings over his breast pocket. Combat soldiers don't wear identifying marks on their uniforms out in the boonies, no insignia of rank like stripes or bars, nothing beyond a name tag, nothing the enemy could exploit right away if he captured you. I think I'm going to like this guy, I thought. He surely faced the same danger as I had "out there" in the not too distant past, only he bore the additional burden of command. He had already earned my respect by the way he comported himself during the ambush, the way he rallied us into action, the way I saw him look at Jake Lambert before they shrouded him in his poncho for the dustoff. I couldn't judge the depth of the relationship between Troy and his radioman, fact is, I figured it was none of my business. Nor could I guess the impact war deaths had on this Airborne Ranger.

"Private Calloway," Lieutenant Troy said calmly, not realizing—certainly not caring—that he had interrupted my train of thought which had begun the process of proclaiming him my first honest to goodness war hero.

"Sir."

"Private Calloway, the world lost a truly good man the other day."

"Bingo," Sergeant Smith interjected on impulse, throwing military protocol out the tent flap. "Jake Lambert was the best."

"Where do you come from, Private Calloway?"

"New Jersey, Sir."

"I say the world lost a good man, Private Calloway from New Jersey, because for better or worse, for you, for me, for Sergeant Smith here, and for all the rest of us in this outfit the world has shrunk. The world is not New Jersey, or California, or the North Pole, or Timbuktu. The world is this place, Vietnam, and this place is at war." He paused, looking at his cup. "Jake Lambert was a good man."

"The best," Smith agreed again.

"I'll come to the point. I need a new RTO and you're the man."

I babbled something perfunctory about my ignorance of radio-telephone operations and inexperience, to no avail. But, hey, this is the first time anyone in This Man's Army referred to me as The Man.

"Sergeant Smith, I realize this will leave you a rifleman short again, but wherever the RTO comes from leaves that squad short. Private Calloway, being new to the platoon . . ."

A whistling overhead caught the immediate attention of Troy and Smith. And me, beginning to pucker. Then the blast. The mess tent shook momentarily as the shock wave rumbled through it. "Incoming," someone outside yelled. "Incoming," several frantic voices echoed in stereo. Everyone inside the mess tent sprinted out of it and I dove into the first ditch I saw, which just happened to be the one dug around the tent that housed second platoon's first and second squads. Tommy and Eddie were already there, and I guess the rest of the squad was there too; but I wasn't counting noses, just ducking.

Realizing that we were under mortar attack and having raced from the mess tent to the ditch dug for exactly this purpose, I could now feel my heart beating wildly. The twenty-five yard—er, meter—dash and dive left me panting. "Relax," Tommy said, he already sitting in the hole. "Here, I brought an extra can of soda." "They're bombing us," I whispered at the top of my voice, not wanting to give away our position to those rotten VC who had the nerve to attack our base camp in broad daylight, "and you want me to have a can of soda?" "Yup," my self-appointed mentor said with incredible nonchalance. "Number one, ain't nothing we can do about them shells right now, and B, you can talk normal 'cause Charley can't hear a word you're saying from wherever he's popping them mortar shells, anyhow." "Roger that," Eddie agreed in Armyspeak.

Concerned primarily with my own safety during the attack, I marveled later at the actions of those around me. First, of course, was the devil-may-care attitude of Tommy, Eddie, and the rest of the guys in the ditch, three of whom actually brought their pinochle game with them. Sergeant Smith and the other noncoms scurried about the area checking to make sure that all of their troops were accounted for. Lieutenant Troy hadn't even bothered jumping into the ditch as Smith and I had, but rather ran directly from the mess tent for about sixty or seventy meters beyond our squad tent to the bunker that served as the battalion tactical operations center (BTOC). A short time later, by the time Tommy had convinced me to take the can of soda, Troy appeared standing—not crouched, mind you—standing in the waist-high ditch, getting an accounting from his squad leaders. "All here, Sir," Smith reported. "I don't like this new world very much," I said to myself under my breath, "but I sure like the guys on my side."

Back to School

"The hard part ain't operating the radio," Spec-4 Marchetti said in summation, "or even lugging the bugger through the woods. Nah, the hard part is anticipating what your Six wants."

Lieutenant Troy did not reconvene our meeting after the mortar attack, which consisted of four sporadic rounds, none of which hit anything of substance, thank God. He must have met at some point with Sergeant Smith, however, because Smith sat next to me at chow that night and repeated Troy's earlier words: "You're the man." He told me there was no hurry to move my gear out of the squad tent, not until another replacement arrived, anyway, but I was to get together ASAP with Marconi, one of the two company RTOs, and get smart fast on the PRC-25 I would be humping through the jungle from now on.

"Troy's right," Sergeant Smith said. "Even though I can't afford to give up a rifleman, especially an experienced one like yourself," he kidded, "the platoon can't operate at all without an RTO. I probably lost you when I told Troy that you held your own during that ambush. You fit in real well with my squad, Calloway." I wasn't sure he was still talking about me, seeing as how I had a tough time remembering details of the incident. "Now you need to prove me and the lieutenant right. Be the man, Nick!"

"Six is the man in charge," Tony Marconi instructed. "Next down the chain of command is five. So, for example, at battalion, Colonel Hernandez is Gimlet 6, his XO (the executive officer) is Gimlet 5. The company commanders are Alpha 6, Bravo 6, Charlie 6, and Delta 6; their XOs are 5s as in Alpha 5 and so on." No abstract algebra here. "At the platoon level," he went on, "it goes like this: First Platoon Leader of Alpha Company is Alpha 1-6, Second Platoon Leader is Alpha 2-6, and so on. Got all that?"

"Roger," I replied half jokingly because present circumstances did not require radiospeak, but also half proudly because I realized that I had picked up and drifted into the lingo rather easily. I was beginning to think of myself as The Man, not that man who had his own army like Sir Sergeants at Dix and Polk, mind you, but nonetheless a man with a real purpose in this shrunken world I found myself in. "Something's bothering me, though, Tony."

"What's that?"

"Jake Lambert," I said. "Tommy told me his call sign was Jenny 4. He picked it out himself and insisted that he be known as Jenny 4. What was that all about?"

Tony brought me to the company headquarters enlisted staff tent about a hundred meters deeper into the compound, not far from BTOC. "Jake bunked over there," he said, pointing to the far corner. "We haven't packed up his stuff yet. Nobody's in a hurry to say a final goodbye to Jake." As we walked toward the fallen RTO's area, he told me quite matter-of-factly that I would not only be assuming Jake's duties, his area would become mine, too. I couldn't figure why Tony thought it necessary to take me to Jake's corner, and then, just as curious to me, when we got there he sat himself down at the foot of Jake's unruffled cot.

"Open his footlocker," he said, like he was inviting me to unwrap a birthday present. "Go ahead. It doesn't matter to Lamb now, and it wouldn't have mattered to him if he were here. In fact, he'd want you to open his footlocker."

"Neat," I said. "Everything's so neat."

"And right there on top, on the right side, is Jake's bible, right?" He wasn't looking at the footlocker when he said this. Strange.

"Right."

"He wanted everybody to know it was there. 'Just go ahead and borrow it anytime you like,' Jake told us. Funny, you know, at one time or another we all took him up on the offer."

It's hard to explain the immediate effect of the scene: Tony Marconi sitting on Jake Lambert's cot, hands folded and resting on his lap, eyes staring at the dirt floor, and me kneeling at Jake's open footlocker, holding his bible. I should have felt uncomfortable. I didn't. This surely wasn't a holy place by any dictionary definition. And it's not that uncommon for soldiers to carry bibles in a war zone. Yet the way Jake Lambert left his area before going into the field for what turned out to be his last mission left an aura of dignity, solemnity, perhaps. I just cannot describe it.

"Open the bible to where Jake placed an airmail envelope," Tony said.

It was Genesis, Chapter Four, the story of Cain and Abel. "I don't get it."

"It's that one line there, the one he underlined in red." I read it aloud: 'Am I my brother's keeper?' Lamb loved that line. He lived by it. 'Yes,' he would say. 'I am my brother's keeper. And so are you.'"

"But the call sign," I asked. What was that all about?" I figured that Jenny was Jake's girl back in the real world and I kind of conjured up this romantic notion of him loving her so much that he wanted to keep Jenny with him all the time. I mean, isn't that a big part of what war is all about, you know, having someone special waiting at home for you, writing letters twice a week about all those trivial things that mean so much when you're away, sending "care" packages every now and then with homemade chocolate chip cookies to share with your buddies? But I digress once again.

"Well," Tony said, "it was kind of an inside thing. Just within the company, you know?" He explained that when Jake was assigned as RTO for Lieutenant Troy about four months before he requested that he be known over the air as Jenny 4. The other RTOs didn't know the story at the time, the biblical reference, that is, but apparently Jake convinced Troy to let him have the handle.

In strict Armyspeak the number four—G-4, actually, G for staff at the division level—designates the logistics officer. At the company level, there was no such breakdown; six was the CO and five his XO; the numeric code didn't go any deeper than that. "Okay, Jenny 4 it is, then." Troy had given his blessing and the call sign stuck.

It wasn't long before everyone in the company, and most of the RTOs in the battalion for that matter, knew that Jake Lambert was Jenny 4. Hardly anyone knew exactly what that really meant but they seemed to like the military slang ring to it. "Hey, Jenny 4, how's about passing down that mustard?" "Roger, wilco," he'd reply, or "on the way, wait." "And then a funny thing happened," Tony said.

The platoon pulled base camp bunker duty not long after Jake became RTO. He happened to be in the BTOC when the brass was trying to come up with a password for the night. "I've got one," Jake said. Taken a bit aback for a moment at the enlisted man's pluck, the officers looked quizzically at each other. "Okay, son, Gimlet 5 said. What do you have?"

"The challenge will be 'Halt! Who are you?' The response will be 'My brother's keeper.'"

Another pause in the bunker as the group looked one to the other. "Why not?" the XO, Major Baldwin, said. "I like it. Who are you," he asked Lieutenant Troy who sat directly across the table from him. "My brother's keeper," Troy responded with no hesitation. "Who are you," he asked each man present at this impromptu pep rally that Spec-4 Jake Lambert inspired. "My brother's keeper." Loudly, "My brother's keeper." Proudly, "My brother's keeper." "Yeah," the XO said with a smile, "I like it."

The slogan unified the company after that. "Who are you" any soldier of any rank would say to an approaching comrade of any rank within the confines of the base camp. "My brother's keeper" came the immediate reply. At first it seemed little more than a catchy use of the language that allowed privates and Spec-4s to speak as equals to noncoms and officers. Then it stuck.

JENNY 4

Every man in Alpha Company, Three Twenty-one believed he was, and therefore acted as, his brothers' keeper. Jake Lambert, Jenny 4, lived on in all of them, and now in me.

Chapter 6

January 1967: Mail Call

> "As cold water to a thirsty soul,
> so is good news from a far country."
> Proverbs: 25

Mrs. Calloway
305 Ann Street
Harrison, NJ

PFC Nicholas Calloway
"A" Company, 3/21
196th LIB, APO San Francisco

Mail Call
Dear Nick,
Thanks for the letter. We love to hear from you, even though we're not sure what your job is over there in Vietnam. Daddy keeps watching the news every night at 6:00 and 11:00 o'clock. He used to go to bed at 10:30 but now he watches the late news every night. Sometimes I watch it with him, but to tell you the truth I don't like to. When news of the war comes on we kind of hope we see you on the television. But really I'm not sure I want to see you that way. The boys we do see all look so young. Daddy doesn't say much about the war. You

know him. Aunt Patty and Uncle Pete came over for dinner the other night. Uncle Pete said he was glad there was no war going on when he was in the army and he told us all about how nice he had it over in Germany. After they left, Daddy said it wasn't so great when he was in the army in Germany during World War II. He doesn't talk much about that to anyone, not even me, so I guess that's where you get it from. He did say though that Uncle Pete is lucky being the youngest brother because he got to go to college on the GI Bill but didn't have to fight in a war first. Do you think you might go to college when you come home? I think you would be a great teacher and teachers have job security and you can have summers off if you want to play with all those grandchildren you're going to give me. I hope you don't have to go back to the factory. Anyways, I know it must be hard to write sometimes but please drop a line whenever you can. We're all praying for you and for all our boys over there. We want you to come back safe to us. We love you very much.

All my love,

Mom

P.S. I almost forgot. Aunt Patty introduced me to a lady the other day from Kearny named Mrs. Cox. Her son Adam went into the Army the same day as you. He didn't go to Louisiana though for training, she said he went to Fort Meade. Daddy says that's in Maryland. He's in Vietnam too now, but I don't remember where she said. Do you know Adam?

M. Troy
1019 Grove Street
Oak Park, Illinois 60304

1st LT Joseph Troy
"A" Company, 3/21
196th LIB, APO San Francisco

My Darling Joe,

I miss you. I miss you. I miss you. I know I shouldn't burden you with how much I miss you, but I can't help it. I'm so glad I went back to work in September because the only thing I have to concern myself about during the day is twenty-three third graders, instead of worrying about you all the time. My wonderful memories keep me going, but I don't want to live only in the past.

I remember how proud of you I was the day we graduated, you getting your gold second lieutenant's bars and all the ROTC guys looking so much more mature in their uniforms than the "regular" grads. Best of all, you were mine, all mine, that was the sweetest part. I didn't even mind that you were going off to ranger school just one month after the wedding in June because that meant so much to you and, anyway, Soldier Boy, I knew you were coming back to me.

Little Joey salutes every time he passes your picture on the coffee table. He's so cute. "That's my daddy," he says. I say, "Who are you?" He says, "I'm Daddy's big boy." I know every mother in the world thinks her child is the brightest and cutest and all that. But, Sweetheart, our boy is all that and more. He doesn't know that I have made it his job to comfort me, to make me feel safe, to bring joy into my heart when I feel lonely. That's an awful lot to ask of an almost three-year-old. He does it, though. So often I look at him and see you. No matter where we are or what we're doing, I find myself staring at our beautiful baby boy and thinking how wonderful it makes me feel to know he is a product of our love. Dr. Cotler insists on seeing Joey once a month. She's so conservative.

Your letters make me angry, sometimes. You always ask what we're doing, but you hardly ever tell me what's happening in your life. Every now and then I walk in on a conversation in the faculty room or the cafeteria. The other teachers grow silent. They're talking about the war, I know, and they don't want to upset me. It wouldn't upset me. I don't care about the war, Joe. I should, I know. I only care about you coming home. I want you to come back safe to Joey and me. He needs you. I need you.

Your mom stayed for dinner last night after she brought Joey home and we had a really nice talk. We put our boy to bed and sat at the kitchen table over a pot of tea. I told her about how you and I met junior year in American Lit. The professor sent us off in small groups one day to talk about Hemingway's *A Farewell to Arms*. Oh, Joe, I was so happy to be with you. I told your mom I had a crush on you since the first day of class and, as soon as Dr. Richards told us to get into groups, I wiggled myself right over toward you. You never had a chance after that.

Your mom wanted to hear the whole story and I needed desperately to relive that happy memory. I know you remember, but I want to write it down. I told her how you and I agreed on everything about the story, especially about the characters. Class ended. I wanted it to go on forever. Then, the handsomest boy I ever met asked if I would like to talk more that evening about Hemingway and World War I and expatriots and who knows what else you said. "I guess so," I said, not hearing much after "talk more," and trying not to seem too anxious.

Joe, I know this sounds dumb, but drinking cup after cup of tea with your mother in the kitchen reminded me how easy it was to sit with you for hours that first "date" in the commons, drinking so much coffee I couldn't sleep at all that night. (Okay, I'll admit it now, I was pretty excited about my new boyfriend, even though you didn't know you were my new boyfriend at the time, and I probably couldn't sleep that night if I was on tranquilizers.) We concluded—sophisticated college students as we were—that some wars are just, WWI being one of them. You got a little pompous talking about the hero code and then the shallowness of Hemingway's women. "And here," I told Mom, "is the precise moment I fell in love with your son." You made a point—a very good point—then you listened to mine. You always listen, Joe, and I like that very much.

Catherine Barkeley did say some silly things in *Farewell*, I conceded. She dreamed romantically of her fiancee going off bravely to the war and coming home triumphantly with a slight saber wound. The poor fellow got blown to bits. I admitted to you that her attitude was indeed naïve—you're word. But you heard me out, you looked straight into my eyes; our fingers almost touched across the table. Oh, how I wanted you to hold my hand. You came to see my point of view that naivete and romanticism about war and its consequences were not restricted to females. In fact, we talked ourselves into the opinion that ignorance and idealism "in males" often cause wars to be fought in the first place.

Oh, Joe, I love you. I'm not Catherine Barkeley and you're not Frederic Henry. I don't want you coming home with medals for bravery. I don't want you coming home with one of those Purple Hearts. I don't want you coming home like your dad did from the Philippines, never able to talk to his own wife about two whole years of his life. I only want you home in my arms. I want you in my life, every day.

I love you. I love you. I love you.

Forever Yours,

Marianne

Chapter 7

February 1967: Chopper Down

> "And I said to the man who stood at the gate of the year: 'Give me a light that I may tread lightly into the unknown.' And he replied: 'Go out into the darkness and put your hand into the hand of God. That shall be to you better than light and safer than a known way.'"
> "The Desert," M. Louise Haskins

"Here's the situation as I know it." Lieutenant Troy was standing before the second squad, me included, as we sat at two of the picnic tables in the mess tent. No pleasantries, this time, no offer of coffee, no iced tea. It was 0630 and he was wearing freshly laundered, not starched, jungle fatigues, shirt sleeves rolled evenly just above the elbows, pants bloused smartly inside his jungle boots; no sign of rank, however, no ranger badge, no paratrooper insignia.

The company rotation of duties had us sleeping comfortably in our tent under mosquito netting the night before; no bunker line, no ambush, no ditch diving to duck incoming mortars. We now sat before our platoon leader in various stages of undress—an odd scene, I thought—because they didn't begin to serve chow until 0700 and most of us were still moping around the tent area when Sergeant Smith gave the word to drop everything and hustle on over to the mess tent. "And tell who's ever in the three-holer to move it," he said to no one in particular as he exited.

"At approximately 2315 last night, a huey with four aboard went down," Troy reported not quite matter-of-factly but also without any trace of excitement. (I had never in my young life called myself a businessman, whatever that means; but Troy sure sounded businesslike.) "The pilot and one of the gunners were injured pretty bad—we don't know the extent of their injuries at this point—the co-pilot and the other gunner were shaken up. . . ." Troy continued the briefing but his words only served as background noise to the scene playing itself out in my head as he spoke. "No, this isn't Kansas anymore," I thought and then suddenly felt angry, really angry, for letting such a stupid, childish line creep into my brain at a time like this. Troy said that two of the men had made it to safety—I could not focus on the specifics, my mind racing to the crippled chopper, trying to picture the carnage, to visualize the scene, trying hard not to conjure an image that included shredded human flesh— ". . . and second squad, second platoon is going to bring back those two American soldiers."

Nothing registered, and everything registered. As I listened intently to Lieutenant Troy—trying to, anyway—my eyes drifted to two Vietnamese men wearing American style jungle fatigues sitting at a table close to the empty chow line. One—the older of the two, perhaps in his mid-forties, although I couldn't really tell—sat almost trance-like, staring straight ahead, cradling a coffee cup between both hands. Very strange; he looks like my father, I thought; particularly strange since my father is of Irish descent. The other, a man maybe a little older than I, seemed riveted to Lieutenant Troy's briefing.

I guess I was getting the main drift of what Troy had to say. Most important, and weird, though, I began to feel a sense of pride welling up inside me—not arrogance, but a prideful air of self-importance; confidence, maybe. No, camaraderie; that was it. I was part of a team: this team, this outfit. This brotherhood. My being in Vietnam right now, right this moment, had a purpose. Unlike the occasion of my baptism by fire a few short days ago, protected then by my innocence, this time I knew the mission. I sat in on the briefing, for heaven's sake, with my . . . with my brothers. Two GIs we never met lay wounded and stranded in this microcosmic world at war and I was going to take part in the search and rescue mission that would return them to safety, maybe even expedite their return to the "real" world. We weren't going to ride in on white horses, pistols blazing. But we sure as hell were going to . . .

"Sergeant Smith, have your men draw ammunition and C-rations for a couple of days. I can't say how long this mission will take."

"Yes, Sir."

"And listen up, all of you." He hardly needed to say this, he already had our attention—I mean, I may have been day dreaming a little, but I was still paying attention. "Take only the entrees. I don't want any crackers, or coffee, or cigarettes out there. No Kool-Aid in the canteens, just fresh water. Sergeant Smith."

"Sir?"

"Soft caps and camouflage skin paint. One entrenching tool and one machete per fire team. And every man carries two grenades minimum. Liftoff will be in approximately one hour and fifteen minutes."

"Yes, Sir. Anything else?"

"Just one more thing, Smitty. I'm going with you."

All of this took less than five minutes. As we began to leave, Lieutenant Troy told Sergeant Smith to stay a minute. "You, too, Private Calloway. Hang on." He continued in this incredibly understated tone of authority for a man I guessed to be no older than 23 or 24, "I want you both to meet me at BTOC at 0715. Nick, you're my RTO. Don't weigh yourself down with too many magazines and forget the grenades, that radio and spare battery will be enough for you to carry."

"Roger that," I said, falling immediately into character.

I was excited and nervous, not pucker nervous, more let's-get-out-of-the-locker-room-and-start-the-game nervous. What do I do first? Better grab two slices of that toast sitting at the end of the mess line the cooks and KPs laid out while Troy was briefing us; don't know when I'll eat real food again. Sure glad I had already hit the latrine before Sergeant Smith mustered us. Hustle back to the tent. Funny how there was no need for anyone to scream, "Move it, move it, move it," anymore. The Man at Dix can keep his army, and so can the one at Polk. I'll take this one.

"Entrees," Tommy said with an expression somewhere between a sneer and incredulity. Number one, ain't nobody in the real world could ever call this dog food a meal, and B, entrees?" He received no disagreement as we each loaded a black or green sock with cans of ham and eggs, lima beans and ham—yuck—meatballs in tomato sauce, and chicken and noodles. The idea was to tie the sock to the cross piece of the harness in back, allowing it to dangle noiselessly during jungle transit and then shrink, one meal at a time. Carrying our food this way also left room in the rucksack for more ammunition and dry underwear and socks.

I watched Tommy perform another packing-for-the-field trick, then imitated it with no need to have him explain. Each C-ration box contained plastic utensils wrapped in cellophane. After placing several in his pack, Tommy opened a package carefully at one end, emptied the knife, fork, and spoon onto his cot, and slipped the package over the barrel of his M-16. He reached into his pocket, opened his hand, revealing several small rubber bands, tossed two in my direction, and without saying a word secured the improvised dust cover over the open end of his weapon.

"Voila," Tommy said with an almost grin. "Number one, no dirt gets in; number two, no rain neither; and C, barrel stays clean as a whistle."

"C'est magnifique," I replied, meaning of course to congratulate him in the lingua franca he had chosen to celebrate his feat.

"Huh?"

"Thanks for the rubber bands," I said.

"No sweat."

BTOC, The War Room

When I entered the BTOC, neither Lieutenant Troy nor Sergeant Smith had arrived yet, although several other officers and senior noncoms from the company stood around chatting. "Here you go, Nick," Marchetti said as soon as I entered the bunker. "Your radio is all set. I calibrated it for you. Take it outside and we'll give it a test."

"Roger."

"Reminder, Nick: Lieutenant Troy is Alpha 2-6, Sergeant Smith is Alpha 2-5, and for purposes of this patrol you are Alpha 2-4. We're keeping it real simple."

"Copy."

The radio tested fine and I reentered the bunker. By then Troy and Smith were sitting across from Captain Hurley, Alpha Company Commander (Alpha 6), Colonel Hernandez, the battalion commander (Gimlet 6), and Major Baldwin, Hernandez's XO (Gimlet 5). "Sit down over here, Nick," Lieutenant Troy said, tapping the chair next to the one he occupied. "You need to hear this." The others, platoon leaders and platoon sergeants, were already seated at the table next to ours.

In less than a month in this topsy-turvy world at war, I had survived an ambush, saw a man's skull explode, had a sergeant and a lieutenant tell me I was The Man. And now I was about to sit in on a battalion-level combat strategy session. Maybe I really am The Man. Nah! Not yet.

"After the crash, Lieutenant Sullivan and Specialist Nash made it safely through the brush during the night. At approximately 0500, they reached an ARVN camp about three clicks north-northeast of the crash site. They knew it was there and had headed toward it. They contacted us from there." There was a little fidgeting in the room. "In case you're wondering," Colonel Hernandez continued, "the pilot, Lieutenant Richardson, ordered them to go. Richardson and his gunner, Specialist Irvin, stayed with the chopper. Apparently both sustained significant injuries, but we don't know how severe. They were alive. They were armed. They lost radio contact when the bird crashed. At this time, that's all we know. And," he added, "we've also lost radio contact with the ARVNs. Something bad is happening out there."

He told us that another meeting was taking place "right now" over at the 2nd of the 1st. "They're going to drop a rifle platoon near Fire Base Bravo and bring back Sullivan and Nash and try to find out what the hell is happening." They had their mission. We would have ours.

Colonel Hernandez then gave a quick synopsis of the events surrounding the crash as best he could reconstruct them, stating unequivocally that of utmost importance was the mission at hand and how he planned to have us accomplish it. He explained that the chopper was part of a routine harassment patrol last night, gunships flying as close to the tree tops as practical with machine gunners firing short bursts sporadically. It didn't matter if there was an actual target or not. The entire area had been designated "black," that is, it was considered enemy-occupied. Black areas were also called "free fire zones." This is what happened.

While making passes over the assigned area, Richardson saw a small clearing and decided to check it out. Nothing but foliage visible. The gunners sprayed a few rounds. No response. They moved on. A short time later as all choppers were returning to base, Richardson decided to approach the clearing from the opposite direction to get a different look. Again they saw nothing. The gunners didn't even fire this time. Suddenly, a blast from below. The chopper shook violently and jerked, tail up, nose down. The bad guys—"We don't know whether they are VC or NVN regulars," Hernandez said—set off an antitank mine, a Chinese Claymore, aimed at the sky, a common enemy defensive tactic against low flying helicopters.

"As best we can determine, because of their altitude, and because the hit occurred over the small clearing, the chopper banged into the tree line, probably hitting pilot side first."

"That accounts for Richardson and Irvin taking the biggest whacks," Lieutenant Troy said clinically.

"That's what we figure," Baldwin agreed.

The Plan

Colonel Hernandez rose and stood at the map pinned to the wall behind him. "Time is as treacherous an enemy, right now, as Charlie himself." He told us that gunships hovered over and around the site all night but could not attempt an extraction because of the darkness. Moreover, he said almost apologetically, maybe even embarrassed, we have no idea of the size or overall capabilities of the force out there and without intelligence could not risk a night drop of grunts. Then, solemnly, he said, "The chopper jockeys report no sign of Richardson or Irvin. They've had search lights on the wreck most of the night. They have eyeballed it since sunup."

My mind flashed back to the moment of Jake Lambert's death. He died instantly. There's mercy in that, I thought.

Richardson and Irvin were alive when Sullivan and Nash left them. Are they still there? Alive? Dead? Did they escape into the jungle? Did they bleed to death? Did one perform mouth-to-mouth resuscitation on the other? Oh, God, Sir, get on with it. Let's go. We have to get out there. We have to get them out of there. Open the locker room door. Let us out. Now!

"Lieutenant Troy," Colonel Hernandez began, "this is the plan. Captain Hurley will drop his first and third platoons into the clearing, third platoon first. They will secure the area, set up a perimeter. Your squad will enter with first platoon, on the last sortie." He was tapping the map with his pointer, drawing invisible circles over the crash site. "We don't know exactly when that will be."

"Sir?"

"I told you, Lieutenant, we don't know what to expect out there. If the LZ is hot when we try to inject third platoon, we might have to call in artillery—air strikes, if necessary. We just don't know. In any event, we believe that two rifle platoons are enough to secure the clearing, once they're all on the ground. Captain Hurley, this is your company. Take over from here."

"Thank you, Sir," he said, replacing Hernandez at the map. Tracing an arc with his index finger at each of four points in the clearing—north, south, east, and west—he indicated where first and third platoons would deploy and establish intersecting fields of fire when in position within the woodline. "Yes, Sir." "Roger that." Lieutenants Robinson and Hendrickson marked their clear plastic-covered maps with grease pencil and made sure their sergeants could see exactly where they would dig in. "The chopper is sitting here," he said pointing to the southeast corner. "Lieutenant Robinson."

"Sir."

"When your guys hit the ground, I want you to get a squad into the woodline past that helicopter as fast as possible. Here.

Tell your men they are not, I repeat, they are not to do any rubber necking. No matter what or who they see, they have got to lock in on the perimeter. That is priority one."

"Understood. Sergeant Walton?"

"Understood, Sir."

"As soon as we establish control of the site," Captain Hurley continued, "Lieutenant Hendrickson, I want you to pull one man from each squad, a grenadier would probably be best, and have them rally at the chopper when I give the signal. I'll get there with Alvah (the company medic) and my RTO."

"Yes, Sir." With his back to the map, hands resting on the back of a folding chair, Captain Hurley explained what he suggested was "best case": We drop in to a cold LZ. We secure the area with no enemy contact. We find two happy-to-see-us GIs. We dust them off. And we all come home.

"Let's pray to God that's how it goes," Colonel Hernandez said.

Plan B

I was having trouble figuring where second squad, second platoon came into all this.

"Sir, as I understand it, I'll take my squad to the northwest quadrant of the secured perimeter," Lieutenant Troy said, his index finger touching the spot on his own map, Sergeant Walton nodding agreement. "That's directly opposite the chopper."

"Correct," Hurley replied, indicating the same location on the wall map. "Lieutenant Troy, as I indicated in our meeting earlier this morning, if Richardson and Irvin are not there, your mission is to find them and bring them home." The room grew silent. Colonel Hernandez's "best case" scenario was a pipe dream. We all knew it. Even I knew that the mine that blew that chopper out of the air didn't detonate itself. Charlie sure as hell was out there. And he was armed well enough to drop a couple thousand pounds of made-in-America flying technology into a hole in the jungle.

"Again, gentlemen," Colonel Hernandez took over the briefing, "we don't know exactly what you'll find on the ground, so things might change. But as of right now here's the contingency." He laid out the obvious chain of command: Captain Hurley controls all operations at the site, maintaining direct contact with Colonel Hernandez at the Chu Lai BTOC. Hernandez has immediate access to medevac choppers as well as artillery and air strikes—in fact, I didn't realize it just then, but the artillery forward observer was sitting at the other table and he would be part of the operation. "If all goes well," he said, "we're in and out. If Richardson and Irvin are not there, we will set up a deception."

With the perimeter secured around the downed helicopter, minus two wounded aviators, Captain Hurley would call in a Chinook to lift the wreck out. While that was occurring, we—second squad, second platoon, plus our Airborne Ranger platoon leader, the artillery FO, Sergeant Meenachan, and, I heard for the first time, an interpreter—would scratch ourselves into the ground two-to-three meters apart, facing alternately in opposite directions. Guys from first platoon would then cover us with brush. With the chopper gone, first and third platoons would saddle up and return to base on foot. We would stay.

Nervous? I began to pucker right there on my folding chair in BTOC. The rest of the briefing swirled around me in a haze. Colonel Hernandez huddled with Captain Hurley and Lieutenant Troy, who had dismissed Sergeant Smith so that he could check on the squad's progress. The XO joined the second table where grease pencil-smeared maps defined fire sectors around the perimeter and order of march for the return trip. The interpreters, whom I had not seen come in, sat together in silence by the wall, near the entrance to the bunker.

"Gentlemen," Colonel Hernandez said as he paused to look individually at every man in the bunker, "good luck to you all, and God speed."

Chapter 8
The Wreck

> ". . . it is allowed and necessary to pray to the gods, that my moving from hence to there may be blessed; thus I pray, and so be it."
> "Apology," Plato quoting Socrates

"Move it, move it, move it." The words that sprang from Sergeant Smith's mouth now had a familiar ring to them. How long ago was it that Sir Sergeant introduced us to this refrain at Fort Dix, reinforced by his clone at Fort Polk? The muster of combat infantrymen at the helicopter liftoff area just outside the bunker line at Chu Lai, however, had nothing in common with any gathering of yard birds at the reception center in central New Jersey—nothing—and very little in common with the hurry-up-and-wait school of training we endured in Louisiana. Squad leaders and platoon sergeants literally about to share the dangers their charges would face in the war zone had replaced, thankfully, the spit and polish, loud mouthed, spittle spewing drill instructors who reveled in our discomfort stateside, while they exploited the rank-has-its-privileges axiom for all they could suck out of it.

First Sergeant Tricarico, Alpha Company's "Top," hustled himself along the flight line, passing along chopper assignments to platoon sergeants who in turn divvied them up among the squads. We had begun putting into action the plan briefed at the BTOC an hour or so before. If we were to secure the clearing according to plan—the critical first step in rescuing our comrades, our brothers Richardson and Irvin—we had to hit the landing zone in prescribed order. As Alpha 2-4, I had a front row seat, so to speak, of the scene playing itself out over the air waves.

I heard this chatter, for example: "Alpha 6, Alpha 6. This is Gimlet 5. Over."

"This is Alpha 6. Over."

"Alpha 6, make sure your 1 and 3 are ready to get on that first sortie, and that 2 gets his men in place to board the sixth and seventh birds in the second. Over."

"This is Alpha 6. Wilco. Out." And so on.

I saw the lieutenants passing along instructions to their noncoms and the noncoms carrying out those orders by clustering their squads at appropriate intervals from each other, such that they could board directly into the helicopters as they hit the ground. There was no manifest in the sense of assigned seating on a commercial airplane. But there was a definite order to the proceedings. Troy and I stood near Sergeant Smith and the second squad, and I watched fellow grunts check each other out—a tug on another guy's ammo pouches here to make sure they were attached firmly, there a tightening yank on the flap straps of the now unreachable rucksacks leaning against the small of each man's back.

To an outsider it might seem no big deal, but every now and then I could hear someone ask in a colloquial tone, "Who are you?" The immediate, unabashed reply in monotone, "My brother's keeper."

A few brothers dumped themselves clumsily onto the ground, I guess to ease the burden they would bear for an undetermined length of time once we hit the LZ; but most at the liftoff area stood idly, some dragging deeply on a cigarette. There was noise and motion all around, but not really that much as the squads had pretty much settled in at their positions. I looked at Sergeant Smith and the second squad—

stared probably describes it better—thinking deeply about the unknown circumstances we were about to face. Just as I had heard every word Colonel Hernandez and Captain Hurley spoke at the BTOC briefing, even though my thoughts had wandered inward to my psyche in the middle of it all, I now sensed the panoply of soldiers and gear and dirt arrayed across the dusty gray canvas of the Chu Lai heliport but focused on second squad, second platoon.

Questions. I felt a million questions bombard my brain. I heard every one of them, all at once, yet each one distinctly. Two stood out: Why us? Why me? None of the questions, including these, required individual answers. Not now. The knowledge that Lieutenant Richardson and Spec-4 Irvin needed us bound us. It really was as simple as that. All questions answered within the context of a common understanding that two American soldiers needed us—needed me—to do the right thing.

My world truly had shrunk, geographically and population-wise, and so had my purpose in it. Nothing mattered to me at this moment other than being my brothers' keeper, wherever the choppers dropped us, and wherever we went from there. I know I am not Jake Lambert and I know that Jake Lambert earned the respect of Lieutenant Troy and Sergeant Smith and all the guys and after his death they freely admitted to each other that respect didn't come close to describing the way they felt about him. They loved Jenny 4. No, I'm not Jenny 4, I'm not Jake Lambert. But I am Nick Calloway, Alpha 2-4, and I'm going to be the best RTO I can be and I am going to . . . well, I'm going to do my best.

And yes, I admit it, just then I felt more scared than brave. But, well it's hard to explain, I was scared but not really afraid.

Besides myself, the leave-behind search and rescue patrol consisted of Troy, our leader, Captain Thuoc, the more senior of the Vietnamese interpreters, Sergeant Meenachan, the artillery FO, Sergeant Smith, and the two fire teams. Alpha hadn't been together that long and had recently lost their newest rifleman, me. Buck Sergeant Sam Patterson was team leader, Tommy Hajj, automatic rifleman, and Eddie Vladinsky, grenadier. Bravo was another story worth filling you in on. They were intact, four men: team leader Paddy McBride, automatic rifleman Frankie Fitzgerald, rifleman Tyrone Derkin, and grenadier Johnny Kearns.

What's in a Name?

Pardon yet another digression, please, but I think it's important. Second Squad Bravo Team called themselves the Fighting Irish, which an outsider might think would bother their newest member, Tyrone Derkin, an African-American who came to refer to himself as the Black Irishman. It didn't.

"Everybody listen up," Sergeant Smith said, introducing Ty to the squad in early October. "New man in town. Sergeant McBride, Private Tyrone Derkin will be Alpha's rifleman. Show him around."

That night in the squad tent McBride, Fitzgerald, and Kearns approached Ty sitting on his cot, cleaning his new M-16. "Derkin," McBride the leader said, "we need to talk."

Ty looked quizzically at him. "So talk."

The three—two in tee shirts, Kearns stripped to the waist—sat across from Ty. "It's like this," McBride said. "The guy you're replacing, well, his name was O'Malley. He's the one who started the Fighting Irish stuff. We thought it was kind of silly at first, but then we got to liking it." Ty noticed the leprechaun tattoo on Johnny's right biceps. "We figured that keeping the name he come up with for the team was a good way to remember him." Fitzgerald and Kearns remained silent behind tight-lipped, humorless smiles. "And Derkin sounds

Irish," he said without ironic intent. "What do you say, Derkin? How'd you like to be an honorary Irishman?"

I'm sure Ty thought they were nuts. He was right. Like most of the soldiers I served with in Vietnam, though, it was their craziness that kept them sane. His expression indicated he was considering it. "I got a condition," Ty said, giving each of his new teammates a glancing stare. "If you're gonna call Tyrone Luther Derkin from New Orleans a Irishman, then he's gonna call you his clansmen. That'd make you," Ty said, looking at—not pointing at—Kearns, "Koo Koo. And you, Fitzgerald, you're gonna be Kluxie." They were getting the point. "And, Sarge, since you're the leader, I guess that makes you The Wiz."

Bravo Team, The Fighting Irish, was again a unit, a unified bunch of crazies. Derkin fit in perfectly.

Ty lived for letters from home. Early in December he received a care package along with his usual three or four regular envelopes. He didn't open it, though, until after Christmas dinner in the mess tent. We didn't think that particularly strange, figuring that Ty was exercising restraint in waiting until then to open his gift from home. "Come on, Ty, let's see what you got."

He stripped the heavy tape off the box ever so meticulously, like he didn't want to leave unnecessary bruises on the outer skin of the cardboard. He lifted one flap, obviously enjoying the impatience of the small crowd that had gathered. He slipped his right hand inside, closed his lightly smiling eyes, and grinned a kind of smug grin. "You're killing us, Derkin. Open the box."

With a magician's flair Ty's hand disappeared four times, then one by one he drew out four gift-wrapped boxes with a Santa Claus name tag taped in the middle. "Would there be a John James Kearns anywhere in the house," Ty asked teasingly with a grossly affected brogue. "Ah, there's his self," he said.

"And what does this one say"—dramatic pause—"Patrick . . . Kevin . . . Mc . . . Mc . . . McBride. Is Mr. McBride available?"

"He is," says Paddy. "That would be me self, the beloved offspring of Bridget and Seamus McBride from the clan at Wicklow of the very same name. And a grand and glorious name it is, I don't mind pointing out."

Ty saw his own name on the next tag and set his gift aside. "That would be leaving this final treasure for His Grace, Francis Xavier Fitzgerald, a descendant of kings, as he boasts twice daily from his throne in the privvy, a mere stone's throw down the lane."

"A fine howdy-do is this," Frankie said, "and me not having the time to go Christmas shopping for you, lad."

"Go on, open 'em," Ty said. They did, as did he.

"It's a tam-o'shanter," Paddy said, cradling in his hands the knitted, Kelly-green beret, appropriately accessorized with a pompon in the top center.

"'tis," Frankie agreed, already shaping the woolen crown about his crew cut head.

Ty told his Alpha Team buddies that his grandmother had insisted that he tell her in a letter what he wanted for Christmas. "'Nothing' will not be an acceptable answer," she warned. "Money's usually tight at our house and I didn't want her and Mom wasting money on me," he said, "but Gram loves needle work. 'Idle hands are the devil's workshop,' she always says."

Johnny shook Ty's hand about as hard as he could without crushing it. "It's beautiful, man." Paddy and Frankie hugged him.

Ty's modest attempt at explaining his gifts touched his brothers deeply: "I just figgered that if we're goin' to be the Fightin' Irish' we might's well look the part. So I asked

Gramma if she would knit us up some green berets. I knew she would."

Johnny tried to lighten up the group. His burlesque brogue slipped into a Highlands burr. "Yas know of course, laddies, that the tam-o'-shanter originated in Scawtland." Paddy and Frankie looked at each other, nodded, then said "aye" in unison.

Ty's exaggerated shrug stood as his admission of ignorance to this bit of haberdashery trivia. He propped his right elbow with his left hand, raised right index finger to his lips, and said with a professorial air, "I did not know that. Furthermore, gentlemen, I am quite sure that my beloved grandmama in N'Orleans don't know who invented floppy green hats with balls on top. And I am positively one hunnerd percent positive that them Viet Congs don't care."

"I'll tell you what, Mr. Tyrone Derkin," Paddy said with emotion, "this is the best Christmas present anybody ever gave me. And I promise you, right now, that when we all get back home I'm going to bring every member of the McBride family to New Orleans to meet my brother, his mother, and his grandmother."

That's how tight Bravo Team was.

Back at the Helipad

Bravo wore their tams.

The million questions returned. I deflected them easily and conclusively. "Why us?" "Because, that's all." "Why me?" "Because I am my brothers' keeper." Period. Amen.

"Hey, Tommy. Kinda wish I was back in the squad right now."

"Aah, don't worry about it. Number one, we were a man short before you got here. And B, you're gonna be with us anyhow. Here, turn around and let me check your stuff."

A tug and then another. "Two bladders of water?"

"Yup."

"Spare battery for that radio?"

"In my pack."

"I gotta tell you, Nick," Tommy said as we now stood face to face, "The Man don't just take nobody for his radioman. He snatched Jake outa a squad just like he yanked you. You musta shown him something somewheres along the line."

"I haven't been here that long," I said.

"Maybe so. But A, Troy ain't nobody's fool. That Ranger's as good as they come out in the bush. He gets the job done, he don't take unnecessary chances himself, and he don't like taking casualties. And number 2, he picked you. So you got something he likes."

"I can't imagine what . . ."

"Don't fight it, man. Now tell me, Who are you?"

"My brother's keeper."

"Don't forget it."

There was a low row of sandbags just behind us, probably the first defensive perimeter set up before the base camp of bunkers, tents, and trenches was built. Tommy and I drifted to them to rest without having to settle ourselves all the way to the ground. We sat, he on my right, not talking, just kind of staring toward the lines of troops waiting for their . . . waiting for our transport to the crash sight and whatever waited for us there. I set my left hand on the wall maybe six or eight inches from my body and leaned in that direction. After a moment or two and for no particular reason, I turned my head to the left, glancing toward my hand. A scorpion had nosed itself to about an eighth of an inch from my middle finger. Before I could react to this menacing sight, the beast flicked its tail over its body and stung the back of my hand. "Yow," I screamed, jumping up, grabbing the instantly swollen hand. "Medic," Tommy called instinctively, not actually knowing what had happened.

Captain Thuoc appeared. He took my hand, which now felt like a catcher's mitt, and cradled it in both of his. Although it still hurt, I didn't pull away. He looked at my hand, then rose his eyes to mine. His gaze was gentle, yet penetrating. Comforting. Then, holding my left hand firmly with his own, he raised his right hand to his mouth and spat into the palm. He rubbed the scorpion's point of entry with his moistened hand. Deftly positioning his hands so that our left hands were in a handshake position, he continued to massage the invaded area with his right. He stopped. He maneuvered my hand so that it was now sandwiched between both of his with our fingers in alignment and pointed skyward. He looked into my eyes again. He moved his hands to my shoulders and said, "You be okay, GI."

"Captain Thouc. Nick. What's going on? What's the matter?" It was Lieutenant Troy. "I don't know, Sir," I said sheepishly. "He be okay," the shaman said. Without explanation, without expression, he walked away.

Takeoff

"Alpha 1-6, Alpha 2-6, Alpha 3-6, this is Gimlet 5. Acknowledge in order."

Troy was close enough to me to hear the radio traffic. He reached for the handset clipped to my harness and waited a moment.

"This is Alpha 1-6. Acknowledge. Over."

Troy repeated the response, then handed me the handset which I reattached chest high to my harness strap.

"Alpha 3-6. Acknowledge. Over."

"This is Gimlet 5, Gentlemen. Birds will be landing in approximately five minutes. Second sortie ten minutes after that if all goes well. You will not hear from me again until you are airborne and only then if the scout choppers reconnoitering the LZ report enemy activity. Good luck. God speed. Out."

"Relax, Nick," Lieutenant Troy said. "We're hopping the second train. We've got some time. You're going to be all right."

I guess I believed him. I wanted to believe him. He had this way about him that allowed Sergeant Smith to interrupt him in the mess tent without showing any sign of disrespect. Tommy, I'm convinced, would jump off a cliff into a river full of crocodiles if Troy told him it would be all right. Hey, wait a minute. Do they have crocodiles in Vietnam? Geeze, another thing to worry about.

What, me worry? My radio works. Tommy checked my gear. We had a plan, described in detail at BTOC. We had a mission. We had each other. And for whatever it was worth, I now also had Captain Thuoc looking after me. Nevertheless, I could feel the pucker coming. I gathered myself and looked Lieutenant Troy right in the eye. "Who are you, Sir?"

"My brother's keeper, Nick." He paused as if to let the words sink in, all the while fixing his eyes on mine. "Count on it." Captain Thuoc witnessed the exchange. A slight smile appeared on his lips and he lowered his head slightly as he closed his eyes in a manner that suggested he wanted to respect our private moment.

"Choppers at nine o'clock," someone yelled. They looked like windswept kites in the distance. In seconds the kites morphed into whirling dervishes hovering before our eyes and then waddling to the ground. Before they hit, the camouflage-clad crusaders assigned to the first sortie began their approach to board, grasping weapon in one hand, holding down steel pot with the other. Just like that, they were gone. Ten minutes to go for the rest of us. No turning back—not that that was ever an option.

"Choppers at nine o'clock." Okay, Coach. Open that door. Let's get it on.

"Nick, you stay near me when we get on the ground." Although Troy continued to talk, the thunder of the approaching hueys scrambled his words. I nodded like I heard whatever he was saying figuring, what the heck, I'll sort it out when we get there. Then, just like that, we were sailing above the tree tops.

Do you know how, when you are driving in heavy traffic or through a congested city, you can muffle the outdoor sounds by rolling up the windows? Or if you've ever flown in an airplane, you know how the engines, jet or propeller-driven, create noises so loud that ground crew have to wear ear protection or else go deaf. But inside all you hear is a hum. Let me tell you, riding in a UH-1B helicopter is nothing like either of those experiences.

The huey has no doors to filter out the groaning grrnngg, grrnngg, grrnngg of the engine or the staccato thwopitta, thwopitta, thwopitta of the rotor blades. There is a machine gunner on either side, both of whom are often given the green light to fire at will, a liberty they exercise frequently in free fire zones and in no particular pattern. And yet for all the cacaphonic chaos inside, the view of the war torn Vietnam countryside below approaches serenity: lush green trees and foliage, mud brown rivers, checker board rice paddies. On the way to the battlefield it's easy to forget the war. Well, not quite.

The chopper banks left, begins its descent. Tree tops get closer and closer and we seem to be going faster and faster, an illusion, I know, but that's how it feels. Relax, Nicky. Fight the pucker, baby.

"There it is, Nick," Lieutenant Troy shouted as he tugged my arm, motioning for me to look out the other side as the huey flattened out. Despite the din, I managed to get his gist. ". . . chopper . . . other side . . . radio contact . . .ground . . ." No doubt about it, I thought, this guy is in control. The urge to pucker passed just in time. We jumped out of the chopper—Troy first—before it landed—which it never actually did—raced a few steps, and hit the ground, panting, while the sortie of dragons transformed itself once again into a row of kites gliding toward the sun.

I don't know whether ten minutes is a long time or a short time. But six hundred seconds passed awfully quickly between the liftoff of the first sortie and the approach of the second, I remember. Not much time to think or worry or pray, if I were a thinking man or worry wart or religious person. Having recently turned twenty, a milestone I celebrated with a GI barracks-cleaning party at Fort Polk, I didn't consider myself any of those things. Truth is, I never did much considering about who I was, ever. I wasn't a teenager anymore, even though acne had not yet stopped attacking my cheeks and chin. I'm wearing soldier clothes, heck, I survived a darned ambush; funny though, I don't think I would describe myself as a soldier. Lieutenant Troy, he was a soldier. Sergeant Smith, too. And Tommy. Sirs Sergeant may have been real soldiers once, not anymore. I could never be Troy or Smith. No one could be quite like Tommy. And if I ever saw myself becoming a Sir Sergeant, I'd . . . I'd . . . well, let's just say that that will never happen. Crazy as all this sounds, the concept of who I am began to crystallize; we were all members of This Man's Army, brothers' keepers. So was Jake, God rest his soul.

Where did that come from?

No, I'm not Troy or Smith or Tommy, I'm not Jenny 4. I'm Nick Calloway, Alpha 2-4. That's who I am.

"Nick, get over here. Now!"

We had jumped out of the chopper and Lieutenant Troy had made it to the woodline about thirty yards away. I hit the ground something like a paratrooper, you know, with knees slightly bent to absorb some of the shock and body rolling once or twice continuing the graceful momentum of the jump. I'm kidding. I didn't do any of that, and not one body movement occurred on purpose. This is what actually happened: As my feet slapped the foot-high elephant grass, my body didn't roll forward fluidly, it tumbled sideways under the weight of my pack and radio. I was a half revolution away from impersonating a flipped turtle.

The ten minute head start for the first sortie gave them enough time to insert themselves into the woodline and begin to secure the perimeter. By the time we dropped in, they were pretty much in control. That is to say, they had effectively claimed the clearing as their own with squad leaders already dealing their men into place, establishing interlocking fields of fire from one position to the next. Captain Hurley headed toward the crippled chopper with an abbreviated entourage. I noticed the younger interpreter (didn't know his name at the time) trailing Hurley and his RTO, not thinking much of it at the time, but registering it nonetheless.

"Nick, you have to keep your eyes on me. When I need you, I need you. Got that?"

"Yes, Sir. Sorry, Sir."

I could see Sergeant Smith, the squad, and Captain Thuoc mingled among another squad about ten meters deeper into the woods. Just as planned. God, these guys are good.

"Sergeant Smith," Troy said, "spread your guys and keep them down. Nick, we're going back to the edge of the woodline. I want to see what's going on over at the chopper, and I want to hear the traffic." And that's what we did. So Troy and

I, sitting with backs leaned against the same large tree, listened to the scenario unfold on the radio.

"Gimlet 5, this is Alpha 6. Over."

"Gimlet 5. Go."

"This is Alpha 6. Area secure. No Victor Charlie contact. No sign of good guys, either. Chopper's a mess. Suggest we proceed with extraction as planned. Over."

"Copy, Alpha 6. No need for smoke, we know where you are. Hang tight. Big bird on the way. Gimlet 5 out."

The grenadiers started making their way to Captain Hurley and the chopper. The M-72 grenade launcher is a great weapon in certain tactical situations. In dense jungle, however, it can be near useless or, worse, hazardous to the good guys. Here's why.

The M-72 projects this nifty little bomb—okay, grenade, but a grenade's just a miniature bomb—it hurls the grenade much farther than a Major Leaguer could. Shorter than a rifle, which makes it easy to handle even in the thickest thickets, it breaks open for breach loading just like a shotgun. This is good news and bad news because the round rifles out of the barrel and doesn't arm itself fully until it travels a certain distance. It doesn't explode on contact like a mortar or artillery shell and it doesn't explode after a certain time interval, the way a hand grenade does. This is good because, if the shooter accidentally pulls the trigger and the round hits close by, it will not go off. It explodes only after it has made a fixed number of revolutions; I never learned how many. That's also the sometimes bad news, however. If a round hits a branch, for example, and drops to the ground like a rock, you can't have any idea how close it is to going off. You don't know whether it is one spin away from arming itself or fifty. So you have to leave it (or them) on the ground, effectively land mining your own position.

Grenadiers were issued .45-caliber pistols so they could defend themselves in situations where launching grenades doesn't make sense. However, although a .45 bullet can practically knock down a California redwood, Annie Oakley couldn't hit the tree at any distance beyond six inches with this particular weapon. Conventional wisdom says that, if the enemy is close enough, the best way to take him out with a .45 is to throw it and hope you clock him with it.

Now, truth be told, because of the generally accepted limitations of the .45, grenadiers had the option of turning it in for a twelve-gauge shotgun. Most did. This improved their usefulness as shooters defending a perimeter, but they were still limited to firing two rounds of buck shot and then having to reload. Long story short: The grenadiers were nominated, way back at the BTOC war council, to do the longshoremen's work on the ground of rigging the rubble for removal.

Activate Plan B

Charley was out there somewhere. We knew that, because that's why we were there. And Richardson and Irvin were gone, which is why Troy and our little band of brothers were going to stay. I watched Robinson's group investigate the wreck, checking it carefully for booby traps before touching it or, later when the Chinook arrived, rigging the carry straps for extraction. All the while I heard the back and forth radio chatter between the ground commander and the rear echelon higher ups who controlled our actions in absentia.

No sign of the enemy so far.

Lieutenant Troy had delegated the responsibility of positioning the second squad to Sergeant Smith whom he trusted unconditionally. His sole order was to leave two positions in the middle for himself and me, with his slot facing into the jungle. That left me laying face down most of the time observing the action around the chopper. While our buddies camouflaged us into our shallow holes, Troy stayed near the woodline so he could observe everything. Captain Hurley and his RTO joined Troy when it was time to call in the Chinook. I couldn't hear their private conversation, of course, but it was pretty obvious that the officers were discussing the strategy about to be implemented. Whether or not that's what they talked about, there was no denying the sincerity of their lingering handshake.

Troy made his way to the trench I had prepared for him. "How you doing, Nick?" "Fine, Sir." I expected him to settle in but instead he made his way to every other position checking each man's cover and offering a last word of encouragement. His final stop was with our interpreter who lay on the other side of me. "Captain Thuoc, Sir, you may return to base with Captain Hurley if you like."

"Thank you, Lieutenant. I stay."

Chapter 9

Meanwhile

> "This way for the sorrowful city.
> This way for eternal suffering.
> This way to join the lost people . . .
> Abandon all hope, you who enter!"
> *Divine Comedy*, "Inferno," iii, 1
> Dante

    Of course I—we—had no idea at the time what actually happened to Lieutenant Richardson and Spec-4 Irvin after the crash. It's important, though, for you to know now the terrible things that happened to them.
    Although sore, really sore all over, the pilot's worst injuries were above the waist: a few bruised or broken ribs, separated right shoulder, and a concussion that hurt like hell but didn't render him unconscious. Irvin fractured his right tibia, three inches of splintered bone having pierced the skin at the front of his leg. At the moment of collision with the ground he let out a horrendous, involuntary scream, but pain shock hit him right away, thank God, and he laid next to the chopper dazed and moaning, "Leg, my leg, ooh, my leg." Nash, the other machine gunner, tore the medical kit off the crippled chopper's wall, took out the morphine packet, and injected Irvin just above the knee. The groans elided into a continuous drone.
    After Richardson's "hasty estimate of the situation," determining that Lieutenant Sullivan, his co-pilot, and Nash were well enough to try to make an escape, he ordered them to do

just that. "Get yourselves up to Fire Base Bravo. It's only two clicks northeast. You can get there before dawn."

"Sir," Sullivan said, "you can walk. Nash and I will take turns carrying Irvin."

"Yes, Sir," Nash agreed. "We can't leave you here."

"Can't do that," Richardson said. "We'll slow you down. You need to get out of here as fast as you can so you can come back and get us out of here as fast as you can."

"But . . ."

"No buts. I'm ordering you to get out of here, get to Fire Base Bravo, and then get us out of here. Go! Now!"

If there is one single factor that makes a military unit of any size effective, it is the earned trust that each member has for every other. How else to explain Sullivan and Nash's not-quite-blind obedience to this order? They could have stayed with their pilot and machine gunner—their brothers—disobeyed Richardson's order, most likely with impunity. They didn't. And they didn't choose to obey it because of self-interest or a just-following-orders mentality. Surely their attempted jungle escape through known hostile territory in the dead of night equaled the danger they all might face at the site of the crash.

No. They obeyed Richardson's order because they trusted him. Right or wrong—and who could judge—Lieutenant Richardson was in charge. The order they heard and obeyed was not "Get out of here." It was "Get 'us' out of here." And so, on a mission, they disappeared into the night.

Lieutenant Richardson couldn't recall whether it was five minutes or a half-hour before they were captured. With Irvin broken and drugged and with his own physical limitations, including the piston pounding in his head, he knew the gravity of their situation. I'm only guessing here, but my view is that Lieutenant Richardson had to figure that he and Irvin were in imminent danger of capture, for sure, and maybe death. He had to know that. And he knew that Irvin could not make an escape attempt. In the honorable tradition of the Navy he did not join, he chose to go down with his ship. And more important, in the tradition of all honorable soldiers, he refused to abandon his comrade-in-arms.

And then they came. A squad, about ten of them, Lieutenant Richardson later reported. One grabbed him by his right wrist and another by his left and jerked him to his feet. "Yeaugh!" As two others did the same to Irvin, the dilapidated soldier slumped to his left side, his right shin and foot out of synch with the rest of his body. The morphine stupor wasn't enough to muffle his new pain. Although armed, nominally, they could do nothing to resist. The VC (Richardson assumed at the time they were Viet Cong) tied Richardson's wrists tightly behind his back, intensifying the pain in his shoulder and to a lesser degree his ribs. They prodded him with shoves into the jungle while dragging Irvin several feet behind. Thank God they're not taking us in the same direction Sully and Nash went, he thought, looking for some consolation.

The pain got worse. He thought his shoulder would explode. Can't let them know how bad it hurts. Keep going. Where? Just keep moving.

The captors' point man—God, they're only kids—slithered effortlessly through the triple canopy jungle like a guide at Boy Scout camp. He'd twist his body to avoid a branch or raise his machete to block one in front of his face. He'd no doubt traveled this route many times before. Richardson stumbled along losing all sense of direction as the safari veered left and right in silence. Twice the undulating earth beneath his tentative steps tripped him, the second time spraining his ankle. The tormentor behind him kicked his side mercilessly with his sandled foot. It might as well have been a steel-toed construction boot. No pity. No stopping. If the ribs weren't broken before, they are now, he knew.

God, I can't go any farther. They pushed on. No farther, God, I can't make it. Give me strength. How is Irvin? Is he dead yet? No, I hear his pain. How long have we been on this march? How far have we gone?

The nimble point man disappeared. Richardson, confused and bewildered, stopped. "Ugh." The blunt prick of a rifle barrel in his back forced him to move forward. In an instant, miraculously, when he thought he could go no farther, a man-made clearing roofed with naturally intertwined treetops appeared before him. Three new VC cigarette puffing faces attached to bodies settled in the Oriental squat stared at him . . . and then laughed at the near comatose Irvin whom their cohorts dragged and dropped alongside him in the middle of what he surmised was their base camp.

Dark, very dark, and yet enough shards of moonlight pierced through the foliage to allow Richardson to get a feel for the place. Although not totally rectangular, the area was about twenty feet by thirty feet or so, virtually hidden from the sky.

"Lie down, dog."

The accented voice did not come from anyone he could see. They were the first English words he heard since he and Irvin had begun their descent into hell. "Who . . . What . . . Where . . ."

"I said, lie down, dog. Do not make me angry." The voice switched abruptly to Vietnamese and an animated conversation ensued among the group. "Pete, how are you doing," Richardson whispered.

"No talk. No talk." The already too familiar voice was followed by a stomp on his useless shoulder.

"Ahh!"

"You talk, you die."

JENNY 4

The physical pain in his side and especially in his shoulder had the implausible effect of heightening his sensitivity to what was occurring around him. He had yet to actually see the English speaking face but easily recognized it as the same voice when it spoke Vietnamese. This is the man in charge. Richardson heard the metallic clinking of knives, long knives like the one Point Boy wielded, and was able to see that four of the band had dropped them into a pile. Torture.

The unthinkable thought he had successfully avoided until this moment crushed him. He wept dry, silent tears. His body shook. The gibberish banter continued. The Voice issued an order. Two of his henchmen went to the knife pile. No, no, I'm not ready. I can't . . .

One turned toward Richardson, smiled perversely, and smacked the flat side of the blade against his palm. The American looked away. He stalked his wounded prey with a bully's courage. Our Father, Who art in heaven . . .

The Voice: "On your knees, Lieutenant Richardson."

. . . hallowed be Thy Name. . . .

The Pervert pushed Richardson's head down into the universal posture of submission. Thy kingdom come. . . .

"This time, you do not talk, you die."

Thy will be done . . .

"Look at me."

The Voice's youngish face did not match the gruff sound it produced. Standing rigidly before him wearing U.S. Government Issue camouflage fatigues and jungle boots, The Voice stared menacingly. "You talk now."

"Richardson. Paul. United States . . ."

"Do not play a game with me, Paul Richardson, Lieutenant, United States Army."

. . . on earth . . .

The Voice gestured toward The Pervert who jammed the hilt of his long knife into his victim's skull. Richardson didn't know if he was dead or dying.

. . . as it is in heaven.

The Pervert grabbed the back of his collar and pulled him back to his knees. Not dead!

"Where are the other two?"

"I don't know," he lied and told the truth. "They ran away."

"You stupid man." The Voice continued to talk but Lieutenant Richardson, his brain throbbing against his skull from the last blow, could not follow.

A psychological defense mechanism kicked in and he remembered something very, very strange. When he was a freshman in high school, Paul Richardson tried out for the football team. On the first day of practice an assistant coach lined up all the "fresh meat" into four rows. He told the boys—fourteen years old, fifteen, tops—that he was going to test their courage with a drill called Japanese Suicide. The words alone—courage, Japanese, suicide—intimidated him at the time. What did any of this have to do with playing football? He had no relevant context within which to define, much less understand, courage. The Japanese had something to do with World War II, he was pretty sure, and they made funny little cars that his father said were junk. Suicide?

"In time, Dog Richardson, you will tell me everything." The Voice then lapsed again into Vietnamese.

Give me this day the strength to resist . . .

The Pervert joined two others near the knife pile.

. . . and forgive me . . . Lieutenant Richardson's urge to pray grew stronger; but watching the three soon-to-be executioners, he stalled at the formulaic "as we forgive those who trespass against us." The sight of the man-boys with knives—menacing, ugly knives—drove him toward despair. He slumped to the ground and sobbed. Time passed. He passed mercifully into unconsciousness.

The Pit

Whack. Whack. Thunk. Whack. Lieutenant Richardson awoke to the chopping sound of machetes trimming fresh cut bamboo shoots into uniform lengths. "Pete, are you all right?"

"Leg is killing me. Hope it does . . . soon, Sir," more grunting than speaking.

"You've got to hang in there, Pete. Sully and Nash went for help. The good guys are coming . . ." His words sounded shallow even to himself. "Ugh!" A boot from The Voice forced his face to the ground.

"Dog Richardson, I told you no talk." He paced. "You are going to die . . . Not now. You are going to die when I say you are going to die." The Voice stepped around to where Richardson could see him from the knees down, his camouflage fatigue pants bloused neatly into the tops of his made-in-America jungle boots. The bamboo chopping continued. "Yes, you are going to die, Dog Richardson . . . later . . . not sooner . . . not when you want."

From he knew not where Lieutenant Richardson found the courage to speak. "You know they're looking for us."

"Oh, yes, I know," The Voice replied almost civilly. "And they will find your dead body. I will make sure of that."

Richardson managed to wriggle himself into a sitting position. "And what of my friend?"

"He is already near death," The Voice said, "and do not take me for a fool. He is not your friend. I know he did not want to be in Vietnam, Dog Richardson. His rank tells me he was drafted by your President Johnson's Great Society. He is what the many millions of American students his age call a loser. Yes? Yes." He bent down and looked at Irvin's dog tags. "The last ounce of his A+ blood will fertilize Vietnamese ground. For what?" He stood. "You, however, you are different."

This is not a stupid man, Richardson concluded rather easily, although reluctantly. He is fluent in my language. He knows something of American politics and culture, although just how much is not clear. He knows more about the GI than I do of his military structure. Richardson struggled with his own ignorance of whether he was in the hands of the Viet Cong or North Vietnamese regulars. And where did The Voice get that uniform?

"You call yourself an officer, Richardson, Paul, Lieutenant, United States Army, but you do not lead men. You Americans are an army of cowards. You are a coward. You do not want to fight, only kill." The conversation had ended so the lecture could begin.

The Voice paced left and right, but mostly he stood above Richardson, maintaining his air of total dominance. His rant rambled about the evils of western colonialism: the French in Indochina, the English in India, and now the Americans. He posed several rhetorical questions about imperial motivation, responding repetitively to himself each time, "Greed. Greed, greed, greed." The Voice squatted so that his reluctant student could see his eyes. "Tell me, First Lieutenant Paul Richardson, tell me why you are in my country."

The prisoner knew that spouting out again only the name, rank, and serial number allowances of the Geneva Convention would cause him unnecessary pain. "I am a soldier in the . . ."

"Yes, yes, I know all that. You are a soldier in the United States Army. You are a UH-1B helicopter pilot. Made by Sikorsky, yes? You go where you are told to go. You follow orders."

"I follow orders."

"Tell me, Lieutenant Richardson, who gives the order to kill Vietnamese civilians—women, children, old men? Who gives the order to strip bare our jungle with napalm and plant bombs in our rice paddies?"

No response. Richardson knew this was not an invitation for civil dialog. He also knew that, while, yes, he was a soldier, the more accurate designation was Prisoner of War. He had lost his dignity. He must not surrender his honor.

"I am a soldier, Lieutenant Richardson. I am an officer. I, too, follow orders. I give orders. The difference between us is that, unlike you, I know exactly why I am here in this place right now. This land is my home." His tone softened at "my home" then turned more intense. "You, Mister Richardson, are an invader, you are a pirate. If you had lived, what would you have taken back to your home with you? A trinket, perhaps. Photographs of quaint peasants in rice paddies. Nothing of value. No matter. You will not live. You will not go home."

Had the circumstances been different, Richardson may have attempted to engage this man intellectually. He may even have enjoyed a debate on the ideologies that separated them. "What do you really think of Ho Chi Minh," he may have asked. "Is he the super patriot he'd like the world to believe, or is he a puppet of Russian and Chinese communists?" Although to himself Richardson accepted The Voice's point that Vietnam is his home, he could not concede that the entire population favored some form of socialism over democracy. "The people of the south want us here," he argued in silence. "They asked for American aid. That's why I'm here."

The chopping had stopped some time during the lecture and the woodsmen were now completing construction of two bamboo cages. "Look at your coffin, Dog Richardson. Now you will dig your grave." The Voice unsheathed the bowie knife he had strapped to his belt and handed it to Richardson. "Yes, yes,

I know what you are thinking. You are thinking I will throw this knife at Major Nguyen Ai Quoc. No, Dog Richardson, you will not. You will dig your grave. There." He pointed to an edge of the clearing.

Lieutenant Richardson couldn't recall how long it took him to scrape and hand shovel the three-foot deep ditch. A righty, he had no strength in his right hand. He never passed out, but collapsed of exhaustion several times. Two or three times the ghouls gave him a swig of water. Never did they allow him to rest completely. All the while, Irvin drifted in and out of consciousness. They paid him no mind and gave him no water. When the hole was large enough to hold both tiger cages, as they were called, Quoc The Voice said, "Stop." Too spent to drag himself out, Richardson sank in the hole like a garden hose and slept.

Sergeant Paul Richardson, officer candidate, dreamed a letter he had actually written, so long ago it now seemed, to his fiancee. His dream letter though, the one I include here, contains thoughts he did not actually write to Corrine. The added details of his deep feelings for her then now provided psychological comfort via this temporary sleep-induced escape from The Voice.

Dear, Darling Corrine,
I think of you every day and every night. I hate being away from you. I keep telling myself that it won't be long until you are an officer's wife. I find myself daydreaming often about our wedding day. There we are, you and I, Mr. and Mrs. Second Lieutenant Paul Richardson, running out of the chapel, ducking under the crossed swords of the honor guard outside. I know I'm not supposed to see your gown until your father walks you

down the aisle. Too late, Sweetheart. I close my eyes and see you, white as snow, all the time.

Except for being away from you, Corinne, I am really enjoying Officers Candidate School. It's definitely challenging, mentally and physically, but nothing I can't handle. You know me. When I see something I want, I go for it all the way. I want to be an officer in the United States Army. I want to earn my wings so I can fly helicopters. And most of all I want to hear you say, "I do."

I have to admit, Darling, that all this I want, I want stuff might sound selfish to anyone who doesn't know how much I love you. It is that love that drives me to be the best person I can be. I want (There I go again!), I want so much for you to be proud of me. You see, that picture I have of you and I running the gauntlet of sabers outside the chapel, arms around each other's waist, is the end of "me" and the beginning of "us." Right now I'm only half a person. I know that. The moment I take your hand and look into your beautiful brown eyes and vow before God to love and honor you all the days of my life I will be whole.

It's so easy to love you, Corinne. When we met, I was floundering. You were patient. I didn't want to fall in love with you or with anybody back then. I'm pretty sure I didn't make that great an impression on you in the beginning. Remember that Saturday afternoon I called to tell you I had an overnight pass and did you want to go bowling or something? You were busy. (Pretty nervy of me to call for a date with no warning.) OK, tomorrow then, I said. You made me wait a long time before you said yes. I was running out of dimes for the pay phone. I'll pick you up at 10 so we can spend the day together. Oh, no, you said. That's too early. I'll be in church. I wasn't liking you too much that night.

Even though I had a pass, I didn't have anywhere to go. I slept in the barracks. Well, I really didn't sleep much at all. I kept saying to myself that you knew all I had was a lousy pass from noon on Saturday until 6:00 Sunday night and you blew me off Saturday and then couldn't see me until after church on Sunday. I was glad to see the sun come up so I could get down to the mess hall when it opened for an early breakfast. Then I went to your church, late on purpose, and sat in the back. I watched you sitting with your parents. I'm not sure what the right word is but I think what I felt was envy, because there was something there, something you had and I was missing. Right then I knew I wanted (Sorry!) you in my life. It was a mystery. You were a beautiful, happy mystery. I'm sure glad I went to church that day.

You played pretty hard to get. I tried to act cool. I wouldn't call for a while, figuring that you were sitting by the phone every night waiting to talk with me. That didn't work very well because I didn't know how you really felt about me; but not talking to you, not making plans together for the next time I could see you, was killing me. You were coy. Don't deny it. But you always left me with the feeling that you were falling for me. Maybe I was just kidding myself, I don't know. But that's the way I felt. And after every date I started thinking about the next one. I was falling deeper and deeper in love and hoping you were at least beginning to like me a little.

I realize now, Corrine, that that was only puppy love, if it was love at all. The feelings I had for you in those early days of our relationship were real for sure, but they were childish. I know that now because I had other feelings too at the time. Mostly I was jealous. Whenever I knew you were out with your friends, especially when I had to do soldier things, I got mad inside. I didn't like you socializing or having fun without me.

That's not love. That was the little boy in me feeling sorry for himself.

It's different now, one year later. Don't get me wrong, Mrs. Richardson to be. I miss every minute I'm not with you. But you taught me with your patience that true love means more than holding hands. True love is touching hearts. Being apart doesn't separate us. I'm glad now that you have your family and friends to be with. I know how deeply you care about them. I'm not jealous anymore. You are with me today and always.

All my love forever,
Paul

Prisoner of War Richardson awoke in his cell. During the brief splendor of his deep sleep of remembrance the guards had incarcerated him in the bamboo cage.

Chapter 10
Plan B, Amended

> "Abide with me; fast falls the eventide;
> The darkness deepens; Lord, with me abide;
> When other helpers fail, and comforts flee,
> Help of the helpless, O, abide with me."
> "Abide with Me," H.F. Lyte

Captain Hurley decided unilaterally to abort the extraction plan, after Troy had taken his place next to mine. He reported to Gimlet 5, Major Baldwin, that the frame was in such bad shape it probably would not make the trip back to Chu Lai intact, assuming they could lift it in one piece in the first place. Further, he reported, "the machine guns and ammo are gone."

"Be careful out there, Alpha 1. Charley is better armed today than he was yesterday."

"Roger that, Gimlet 5. Returning to base. Alpha 1 out." With that Captain Hurley gave the order to "saddle up. We're going home." Lieutenant Troy told me to shut down the radio. Just like that, we—second squad, reinforced with a Ranger officer, artillery observer, and interpreter—were alone.

Many thoughts competed for space in my muddled mind as I lay blanketed in foliage. With radio silence now an essential condition of our obscurity I could no longer eavesdrop on battalion banter. Even a whisper between brothers in our current situation was out of the question. I ran through clichés about solitude and rated them against the moment, just to pass the time.

It's lonely at the top. Yeah, I guess so. But I'll have to take whoever said it's word for that, never having knowingly been there, at the top, myself. The top of what, anyway? Are we talking about generals here, or presidents of companies or countries? How lonely can it be at one of those tops, you know, surrounded by sycophants and giving orders all the time? Nah, that ain't lonely at all. That's a small price to pay for a lot of power. On a scale of one-to-ten I'll give loneliness at the top a two.

I seem to recall a book or a movie or something about the loneliness of a long distance runner. Give me a break. Even if trotting through the woods in your underwear for a couple hours every now and then is, almost by definition, a solitary affair, it is self-imposed. Solitary in my book isn't lonely, and anyway it's self-inflicted. Give it a one.

How about people who lose a spouse? Yes, I concede, there is a large dose of loneliness there. But the bereaved have memories. Relatives, most likely, extended family. Friends, too. Support groups. Widows and widowers get a seven or eight. I'm going to make a special effort to visit lonely old people if I ever get out of this little world and return to that big one.

I kept going. Cop walking a beat during the graveyard shift. That could definitely be lonely. Bridge tender. Night watchman at a factory in the middle of nowhere. Cat burglar. Cliff diver. Tightrope walker. Over-the-road truck driver. Hermit. Death row inmate. Duck hunter. Prisoner of war—no, can't count that one; too close to home.

I tried not to judge these individuals. My chief concern, beyond mental exercise, was the degree of their isolation. Was it self-imposed or induced in some other way? Does that make a difference? How does that relate to me? Right now. I took immediate comfort in the fact that I wasn't alone. To my right was a person I already declared a hero. Lieutenant Troy led men in battle, kept his cool under fire, cared about his troops. Yeah, I want him by my side. To my left lay a mysterious man from an alien culture. Captain Thuoc appeared to be a man at peace with himself in a nation at war, a curiously silent interpreter, a man of few words in at least two languages. I'm glad he chose to stay with us. Not exactly sure why—why he stayed or why that affected me. Extended down both flanks are young men who pledge daily that they are each other's keeper, and mean it. They are my brothers. There's comfort in that. Alone with these thoughts, loneliness passed.

Enter thoughts of silence. A sneeze or snore or rustle would give us away. To whom? Where are they? How many? Begin another set of cranial cavity calisthenics.

Silence is golden. So was the egg the fairy tale goose laid. So what? What used camel salesman first convinced a gullible goat herder that gold had value? There's nothing inherently valuable in it for human beings. It doesn't nourish the body, quench thirst, heal wounds; and yet seemingly perfectly sane people trade it for food, drink, and medicine. Crazy. I had trouble rating the silence is golden adage on my scale. The silence part was right up there at ten, no doubt about that; soundlessness could very well mean survival right now. But gold? Pockets filled with gold nuggets would have no value to us. In fact, an errant swivel of a hip could cause the yellow rocks to clunk against each other. Clunk, clunk. Ouch. Here we are, Charlie, come and get us. Okay, what if he does come and get us? We'll pay him off with the gold, that's what. Sure. Wait a minute. Why wouldn't Charlie just take the gold and kill us, which is what he intended to do in the first place? That silence is golden thing is making less and less sense. No rating.

The sound of silence. Oops! Simon and Garfunkel weren't at the top of the charts yet. Scratch that.

Silent partner. That's a good one. Having no idea what the phrase silent partner meant, I ran through a host of partners I knew of and tried to determine how one being silent would add value to whatever it was the pair wanted to accomplish.

Abbott and Costello. Bud often referred to Lou as his partner. Now, would they be just as funny if one of them didn't talk, let's say, during their most famous vaudeville routine? "Who's on first," Bud could say; Lou would shrug his right shoulder and put a dumb look on his face. "What's on second"; Lou would wiggle the left shoulder and pout. Exasperated after several rounds of this one-sided dialog, Abbott would walk away muttering to himself, "I don't understand what's wrong with that guy. If he can't hold a civil conversation with his best pal and answer a few simple questions, why doesn't he just come out and say to me, 'I don't know!'"? "He's on third," Costello would shout out to end the skit. Wouldn't work very well on radio, of course. For a guy laying face down in the jungle hoping an army of ants wouldn't find him, however, it helped pass the time. The Abbott and Costello silent partner act gets a seven.

The Lone Ranger and Tonto. Ah, now we're getting closer. Alone in the Western wilderness with his masked companion in white tights, Tonto had plenty to say. Good stuff, too, like, "When we go town spend wampum on something beside silver bullets, Kimosabe?" Get him into the civilized territories filled with fast talking, double dealing, sons of hopping horney toads, though, and the faithful Indian companion Tonto clammed up like Sitting Bull at Custer's West Point graduation (although he might have let loose a snigger at the valedictorian's prophetic cliche, "This is only the beginning"). Give Tonto an eight on the silent partner meter.

Fred Astaire and Ginger Rogers. What a pair! They actually belonged to my parents' generation of couples to drool at and get giddy over. Musicals, schmaltzy Tinseltown musicals, that was their deal. They floated across the silver screen. Suave Fred sang occasionally to the beautiful, adoring Ginger—I don't remember ever seeing a Fred Astaire record album, however—most of all, he danced. They danced. They danced as one. That's why Mom and Dad watched their movies in reverent silence, to see Fred and Ginger dress up to the nines—a phrase I never understood—and dance. Amid the gaudy glamour of Hollywood's golden age of glitz, Fred Astaire and Ginger Rogers charmed their fans with lithe bodies joined ever so lightly at the hands, romantic rhythm, and their blissful, dancing feet. Either could carry the role of silent partner in the relationship without missing a beat. No words necessary.

I can picture Mom fantasizing herself into Ginger's too-high heels, eyes never leaving Fred's as they glide effortlessly, just the two of them, across every square foot of the grandest ballroom in New York. Or is it Paris? Doesn't matter because it's all Fantasy Land. Dad's interest, though, that's a puzzle. I can't imagine him ever wanting to look, dress, or one-two-three, one-two-three like Fred Astaire, not even with the prospect of holding hands with gorgeous Ginger Rogers. Fred and Ginger get a big tip of the top hat—score that a nine—as silent partners. I can't give them a ten because I haven't a clue what the attraction is for people like my parents. One point deduction for quizzicality.

I realized all along how inane all this was. Maybe even insane. But it kept me awake and alert. Happy thoughts—okay, maybe silly ones—left no room for the demons that would surely have crept into my skull if I stopped long enough to consider the danger I was in. On to another subject for my just-to-pass-the-time trivial pursuit.

Enter professional football players. I'm a Giants fan so I naturally started to list guys on other teams I had to hate for absolutely no reason other than I am a Giants fan. Cleveland Browns, Jim Brown, head of the list, Giants' Enemy Number One. Green Bay Packers, Ray Nitchky, uh, Knitskie, er, Nietche, Knit-ski . . . I hated that middle linebacker so much I couldn't even picture him in my mind because I never bothered figuring out how to spell his rotten name. This hate thing is kind of interesting, I thought. Philosophically speaking, is a man capable of hating another person whose name he can't spell? Forget Whatshisface in Green Bay. Let's say, for example, there were two guys whose names were Jack Peterson and Jack Petersen and you didn't know Jack Peterson but you did know Jack Petersen and you hated him because he played for the Philadelphia Eagles, hypothetically speaking, but you only knew his name from hearing it. You never saw it in writing. See? Well, you're by yourself thinking a pack of bad thoughts about this guy Petersen but as you put the letters together in your head to complete the identification it comes out Peterson. Are you hating the wrong guy? Man, what a waste that would be, philosophically speaking.

Here They Come

A succession of schwish-crack-schwish-cracks along the jungle floor interrupted the playful silence in my mind. Pucker. Get serious. Oh boy! The undeniable sound of footsteps on the grass came from the direction of the clearing, heading left to right toward the wreck. That meant I would see the sound makers before Lieutenant Troy. Before Captain Thuoc. Oh God! Thank God, I remembered, Sergeant Smith also lay facing the chopper. He'll know what to do. I'm off the hook. No, I'm my brothers' keeper. I'm on the hook. This time it's for real.

The instant I heard the first "schwish" my psyche punted despicable Ray Nitchke into sports trivia oblivion, along with every other thought that was not directly related to survival. My body shifted immediately from idle to pucker and every nerve ending from scalp to toe stood at attention. The brain had no time for idle chit chat.

Not many. Moving slowly. Maybe more coming. Troy can't see, Thuoc can't see.

Do they know we're here? No. Can't. Wouldn't be so dumb as to walk into a clearing right in front of us. A little louder, a little closer. There he is. Smallish, thin man. Straw peasant's hat, black pajamas. Weapon? Can't tell. Schwish-crack. Don't move. Don't breathe. Lieutenant Troy, what should I do? The old man stopped and turned. He's waving for someone to come. How many? He's talking with a stern voice. Giving orders? Did he smell us? Captain Thuoc, what's he saying? Schwish-crack. It is a little boy. No sign, no sound of anyone else coming.

Despite the pucker, or maybe because of it, I felt as though I had become an animal: not animalistic; rather, animal-like in the sense that I became acutely aware of Nature. I could smell the difference between blades of grass and leaves on trees, taste again the toast I had that morning. I saw everything. Everything.

Oh my God! Without turning my head for fear of startling the old man, I sensed long, slim, deliberate movement between Captain Thuoc and me. I can't stand it. Snake! It was making a crooked path straight for him. Before I could sort out the challenge to my personal ethics of whether to warn my new older brother of his assassin's presence or try to distract the venomous villain, in the blink of an eye—a span of time played out for me in slow motion—I saw Captain Thouc's fist clenching the now lifeless serpent's neck. Who is this man?

I could hear sweat spewing from my pores, taste the salt. I refocused from the peripheral triumph of Saint George over the leg-less, sleek-skinned dragon to the scene that continued to unfold before me.

It seemed an eternity that the old man and little boy stood staring silently at the helicopter. What must they be thinking? Does aeronautical engineering mean anything to a subsistence rice farmer? To a little boy?

Little boy: Wow! Technology to him is a water buffalo pulling a snaggle-toothed plow. Where does it come from? He's never seen one on the ground before. What magic makes it fly through the air over our rice paddies and trees? Why does my hammock sway when it goes by? Is it dead? It is dead. Why is it here on my land?

Old man: What is this thing, this huge, ugly, awful thing? What sort of man thinks how to make such a thing? Why does any man make such a thing? It flies from there to here, there to here. It doesn't carry rice. It doesn't carry water. It doesn't carry buffalo or pigs. It brings bullets. It brings soldiers from a far away land. It brings death. It causes sadness. What sort of man drives this thing that makes thunder without rain? Why is it here on my land?

I found myself staring at the old man and the little boy in much the same manner in which they stared at the helicopter and realized I had no better understanding of them than they had of it. The helicopter is an invention from a world they could never imagine. I am an intruder in their world, a world I do not understand.

Do they know how poor they are? This old man, older than my father, much older, I'll bet he's never owned a television set or washing machine. Of course not. There's no electricity where he lives. What would he think of Ginger Rogers? Would a vaudeville routine make him laugh? I can't tell if he is a proud man. Does he know that in my country being poor is supposed to be a source of embarrassment? Kids who live in one-family homes mock kids from the projects. Neither of them chose the accidents of their birth. And the parents of born-rich kids teach them to keep the poor kids poor, never to let them get rich because "they're not as good as us." Teachers in America preach all about democracy and freedom and equality. They give tests on all that stuff. But the rich people don't believe any of it, not for a minute. They say they do, when they are kids, to please teachers and get good grades so they can go to the better colleges where they remain insulated from their poor peers; they sometimes say they believe all that stuff when they get older. They don't believe any of it and the rest of us don't believe them when they say they care about poverty and social injustice. They surely don't believe in equality because if all people were equal then they wouldn't be any better than anyone else and that would screw up their entire system of dominance which starts right there in kindergarten.

Did you ever vote, Old Man? I'll bet you never did. That's a big thing in my country. In our system of government, that many say we are trying to get your country to adopt, voting protects us against tyranny and other political plagues like communism. I'll bet you wouldn't vote for that bum Ho Chi Minh. I never voted either, because I'm not old enough, but I'll be able to vote when I get home. Mom's a democrat and she votes all the time. I'm not sure what Dad is. I know he voted for Eisenhower back in the '50s because he still has an "I Like Ike" button in his sock drawer. Eisenhower was a republican. Dad didn't care so much about that, I don't think. To him, Dwight David Eisenhower was a soldier, a man of honor, a great leader who saved the world from Hitler and the Nazis. Just happened to be a republican. Sometimes Dad doesn't vote because he says he doesn't like politicians and most of them never did an honest day's work, he says. Most of them think their job is to keep getting elected, Dad says, so they don't have to do any real work.

Are you a communist, Old Man? If you're not a communist, what are you? Would you be a democrat if you could choose? A republican? What do you think the guy was who thought up the idea of that helicopter that used to have machine guns on its sides? If I was standing in your sandals, except we were all back in the States instead of here in Vietnam, and I was staring like you are right now, I'd swear a communist invented that thing. Guaranteed.

The old man said something, turned, and retraced the steps that brought him to the crash site. The little boy followed. Schwish-crack. Schwish-crack. They were gone.

Loneliness returned. Trivial mind games failed to lift my spirits or fill me with anything useful. All the gridiron heroes and heroics I conjured up shrank to characters in myths. Frank Gifford, Kyle Rote, Y. A. Tittle, Andy Robustelli, Jimmy Patton, Dick Lynch, Rosie Grier, Jack Stroud, Alex Webster, oh, how I loved to watch my Giants on television on Sunday and read about them all week in *The Newark News*. They were the good guys. The Packers, Browns, Bears, Lions, Eagles, Red Skins, they were all bad guys. The morality play *Giants Versus Whomever* acted itself out every weekend in the fall. Us groundlings watched religiously. All across America loyal, mostly parochial fans rooted so hard for their favorite teams that they actually conjured up pure hate for the opposition and, by extension, their fans. And I was one of those rabid rooters. No longer.

All I could think to myself now was, you jerk, it's just a game. Football is just a game. What was the point of wasting energy hating Dick "Night Train" Lane, Chuck Bednarik, and Jim Taylor? If any one of them got traded to the Giants, or had been signed by them in the first place, I would have idolized them for no reason other than they wore Giants' blue. You jerk. None of this has meaning in my new world where this old man lives . . . and I might die.

What if the old man is a communist? My God. Surely that's worse than being a cheese-head Packers fan. Or even a republican. If he is a communist I have to hate him. That's why I'm here, isn't it? For all I know the old man set off the mine that blew up the chopper that carried the brothers I never met. Or maybe the kid did it? Ah, now I'm really confused.

What is this thing, this huge, awesome thing in front of me? What sort of man designs such a thing? What did he have in mind? I realized I had no better clue than the old man and little boy. I wondered about the sheet metal worker on the assembly line I created in my mind; after all, I worked in a ball bearing plant myself, so I knew something about what makes these blue-collar guys tick.

He is union, no doubt about that, a family man: wife, two kids. They live in a house better than they can afford. He works overtime whenever he gets the chance, sometimes he has to but even when they don't make him he always volunteers because he needs the money to live in the house he can't afford. I got hung up trying to assign him to a political party. "Unions always go democrat," Dad used to say around election time. "That's the party of the working man." Yeah, I thought, except this guy—Gus, I'll call him—this guy Gus lives in a republican neighborhood with mostly guys who go to work in tall office buildings in Manhattan: stock brokers, insurance men. "Don't know why they call 'em workers at all," Dad would argue at Uncle Pete. "Brains," would be Uncle Pete's automatic reply. "Takes brains to run this country. Not just muscle. That's what makes America strong: brains."

It never made sense to me why Dad and Uncle Pete never agreed on anything. They argued all the time in the sense that they disagreed with each other about almost everything. They never shouted at one another, though, never showed anger. They just saw the world from different sides, I reasoned. Mom and Aunt Patty usually rolled their eyes during the inevitable disagreements and hardly ever voiced an opinion. Mom came close one time. Instead, she waited until her company left—anyone who came to our house, even Aunt Patty and Uncle Pete who lived right across the street, she considered company.

"He was plumb wrong," she said to Dad. "He shouldn't talk to you that way." Dad didn't say anything, as usual. "It's your fault he doesn't understand why you didn't go back to school after the war. Pete has no idea what it was like for you trying to support our family and giving your mother money every week so she wouldn't lose the house after your father died." They'd been down this road before. "Why do you let him get away with that uppity attitude?"

"He's my brother."

I pictured the Brothers Calloway arguing about Gus.

Dad: "They ought to give him a raise. Then he wouldn't have to work all those extra hours to make a decent wage and do better by his family."

Uncle Pete: "He's the one who wants to live in a big house. The company doesn't owe him anything more than scale. Unions, that's the problem, unions are trying to milk the country dry. More pay for less work, that's all they want."

Dad: "No Gus, no helicopter."

Uncle Pete: "Wrong. There are a million Guses out there. Let him walk. Before he's off the floor there will be another guy named Gus slapping doors on air frames. Investors, they're the backbone of the company, they're the backbone of America. If it weren't for stockholders, there'd be no company. No company, no jobs. Gus would be working the welfare line. Investors, that's what makes this country great."

Dad: "Bull." That was Dad's way of ending arguments with Uncle Pete.

I threw a wrinkle into this hypothetical discussion between siblings regarding fictional Gus the sheet metal worker. The helicopter manufacturer fired him after learning that he was a member of the communist party.

Dad: "Serves him right."

Uncle Pete: "I agree, Brother.

Voice of Reason (Me. What the heck, it's my imagination running wild in the jungle. Let me get into this fight.): "It's a free country, Gentlemen. Gus does his job, pays his taxes. Why can't he be a communist if he wants?"

Uncle Pete: "He can be anything he wants, that's right, Nicky. But that doesn't mean we have to let him work in the defense industry."

Dad: "He could be a spy."

Reason: "If he were a spy, Dad, do you think he would declare openly that he was a communist?"

Dad: "They're sneaky. He could be sabotaging production."

Uncle Pete: "Worse. He could be organizing a strike. Commies don't have any respect for the free market. Lots of union guys are commies, you know. That's right. If they don't get their way—a bigger piece of the profits—they'd just as soon close a factory down."

Reason: "Bull."

Good thing I was lying down, because I was making myself dizzy. I think I just defended a communist. I'm supposed to be fighting communists, stopping the spread of communism in Southeast Asia. What if there is a Gus back home, and what if he is a communist? What if the old man is a communist? Are all communists the same, the way all Cleveland Browns players and their fans are the same: detestable? When foreigners look at Americans, do they see us as all the same? Or do they differentiate between democrats and republicans? Which do they prefer?

I decided to shift the burden of staying alert from my mind to my heart. I composed a letter to Mom, hoping I would be able to remember its contents when I got the chance to write it, knowing of course that I had never written a letter of more than two or three paragraphs. So here's the letter I wished I might write some day.

Dear Mom,
Thanks for the Care package. Everything hit the spot, that is everything I could keep away from my tentmates. The cookies went right away, no way I could keep them to myself. But while the gluttons were pouncing on your now world famous oatmeal and peanut butter cookies, I was able to hide the Slim Jims. They are a real treat. Keep them coming, please.

Mail Call is a big part of our day. Everything stops when the company clerk comes out of the headquarters tent with the mail bag. It's like we all have radar. He doesn't get five steps into the tropical sun and the whole company surrounds him. We look like a bunch of scraggly trick-or-treaters without the masks. And there's always a Care package for somebody, so there's no hiding it.

I'm making some pretty good friends over here. There's this guy Tommy who sort of took me under his wing when I first got here and we were in the same squad. I still see him a lot, but I have a new job. I'm what they call the platoon RTO, that stands for radio-telephone operator. That's kind of funny because I don't really have anything to do with telephones and at home it took me about three weeks to learn how to set my favorite stations on the car radio when I got my license.

JENNY 4

Remember? It's a pretty important job, though. I have to go wherever the platoon leader goes so he can stay in touch with other officers. His name is Lieutenant Troy and we get along fine—as long as I remember that I'm a private and he's a lieutenant. Dad will know what that means.

I was thinking about Dad and Uncle Pete the other day. Dad's a Yankees man, Uncle Pete roots for the Dodgers. Dad's a democrat, I think, even though he voted for Eisenhower, his brother's a republican. Dad puts mustard on his hamburger, Uncle Pete likes ketchup. Is there anything they agree on? Grandma sure had her hands full with that pair growing up. Maybe that's why you decided to just have me.

Aunt Patty sent me a nice letter with a photo of you and Dad standing in front of the Christmas tree. It was really nice of her. She always knows the right thing to say or do to make me smile. I never thought of what Christmas is like in parts of the world where it isn't cold like New Jersey. Well, I can tell you, we didn't have a tree to decorate over here, not even a fake one, but the cooks whipped up a turkey dinner and we all sat around the mess tent for hours singing carols and telling stories about our favorite gifts when we were kids. You know mine, that red and white J.C. Higgins two-wheeler with the battery powered light in the middle of the handle bars. How come you never let me ride it at night? Just kidding!

We get pretty busy around here, Mom. So don't think if you don't hear from me for a while that I'm not thinking of you and Dad. I am. Give Aunt Patty a hug for me and tell Uncle Pete the Yankees are going all the way to the World Series this year.

Love to all,

Nick

P.S. I'm so sorry that Dad and I argued about the war and maybe me having to go. We're both pig-headed, I guess. I realize now that he was only wishing that I wouldn't face the same danger he experienced during his war. He wanted to protect his son, but he knew he couldn't. It's funny, though. Now that I am kind of in his place, I love him more than ever. I'm sorry for the things I said. I'm not going to want my child to go to war either. As usual, Dad was right.

Schwish-crack-schwish-crack. Letter writing time was over. This time the footsteps were louder and there were more of them. Pucker. Five men headed straight for the helicopter. I guessed them to be Viet Cong because they wore black "pajamas" and sandals made out of rubber tires, not military uniforms and boots. They all carried rifles, carbines, I think. One jumped inside and sat himself in the pilot's seat. The others got a big kick out of this and pretended to shoot at him. "Pa, pa, pa," they yelled in the universal language of onomatopoeia, like kids back in the States playing cops and robbers. The "pilot" staggered out of the ship and fell melodramatically to the ground. The rest of the gang hooted and laughed at the charade.

I felt anger for the first time in Vietnam.

Chapter 11

The Enemy Within

> "For here the lover and killer are mingled
> who had one body and one heart.
> And death who had the soldier singled
> has done the lover mortal hurt."
> *Vergissmeinnicht*, Keith Douglas

The enemy band amused themselves like sixth graders at recess in the school playground. Worse, I thought, they are mocking the victims and carnage of war with impunity. To our good fortune, however, they made so much noise they couldn't hear the gentle rustling I sensed up and down the squad. Each of my brothers who had been pointed away from the clearing—and I now counted Captain Thuoc a full brother—managed to reposition themselves undetected. We're going to blow them away any second now.

Pop. Pop, pop.

The single shots, which brought back instant recall of the sniper fire I heard just before Jake Lambert died, were accompanied by a loud, angry, Vietnamese voice. A dozen bad guys emerged from the jungle, about twenty-five meters or so beyond our last man, Tommy Hajj. Only their leader spoke, and he kept shouting at the rowdy boys in black. He fired another round into the air to punctuate his importance and command their attention. Reaching the first reveler, he brushed him aside, then waved the others away from the helicopter, still shouting. His squad demonstrated the discipline of professional soldiers. They walked in a staggered line, several meters apart from each other. When all were in view, without a word or signal from the leader, they formed a tight perimeter around the wreck, each man facing away from it, weapon at the ready—most likely the Russian AK-47s I'd heard about.

The demeanor of this unit reflected their leader's arrogance. They reminded me of a picture I once saw in a magazine of a bunch of hunters on safari in Africa smiling in front of a fallen elephant. Oh, these were the hunters, all right. There's their grotesque trophy.

Scanning the entire patrol of booted men in camouflage uniforms, I couldn't help but focus on two of them wearing bandoleers of 7.62mm machine gun bullets. That meant one thing, and that wasn't good. Yup, there he was, another with an M-60 hanging down his front, anchored around his shoulder with rope. And then I saw another armed the same. Charley's better armed today than he was yesterday.

Suddenly, another loud voice. It came from about the same point in the woodline from where the hunting party had emerged. He walked faster, not quite running, and pointing frantically all around as he continued to shout. He's pointing toward us. Wait a minute. Wait a minute. It's the younger interpreter from the mess tent and BTOC. What the . . .

Lieutenant Troy yelled, "Fire!" In an instant the three enemy soldiers facing our line lay dead. One machine gun toter swung, fired a burst in our direction, and ran for cover behind the elephantine metal prey they had felled the night before—without a doubt it was them. "Bravo, drop a grenade over there." Thwop. Boom. From his position down the line, Johnny Kearns was able to land a round on the far side of the chopper. The human targets vanished as if the M-79 grenade's smoky explosion created a magician's illusion. "Cease fire!"

Sergeant Smith scrambled out of his trench, took two or three steps forward so the good guys could see him, then dropped to one knee. "Alpha, advance to the edge. Bravo, cover. Go!" A few seconds later, "Bravo, go!" Lieutenant Troy called for me and the FO to come to him.

"Calloway, get Gimlet 5. Now! Sergeant Meenachan, I want high explosive rounds on their heads and I want them right now!" Within seconds I had battalion on the air and Meenachan had his map out, ready to plot the artillery fire.

"Gimlet 5, Alpha 6."

"Gimlet 5. Go"

"Enemy engaged prematurely. Unavoidable. Foxtrot Oscar will give coordinates for Hotel Echo barrage. Need it ASAP. Over."

"Roger that, Alpha 6. Put him on."

The squad operated on automatic with team leaders Patterson and McBride placing their men along the woodline. Troy told me to stay with Meenachan while he went up to the line. I watched him signal that he was going out toward the chopper. He ran right at the first enemy corpse and poked it with the barrel end of his M-16. "Sergeant Smith, send two men to check the other side." Fitzgerald and Derkin didn't wait for the order to trickle down. "Stay low," Troy yelled to them, "H-E's on the way."

The two Fighting Irishmen sprinted to the far wood line, right to where the enemy had entered. They fell to their stomachs and emptied one magazine and then another. No return fire. Each crawled behind a tree trunk for protection and stared vigilantly into the bush.

I knelt beside Sergeant Meenachan so he could use the radio. "This is Mean Machine. Over."

"We're ready, Mean Machine. Go."

"This is Mean Machine. Drop one Hotel Echo at . . ." He gave a coordinate. I saw his finger pointing to the target on the map. It appeared too far away, I thought.

"On the way. Wait."

"Everybody drop and cover," the FO yelled. "Drop and cover." In a matter of seconds I heard and saw the explosion about one hundred and fifty meters beyond the wood line. Too deep, I thought. "Stay down," he ordered.

"This is Mean Machine. Three more, same place. Over." Same place?

"Roger. Over." Boom. Boom. Boom.

"Sir," Sergeant Meenachan screamed toward Lieutenant Troy, "we've got the range. I'm going to walk the heat in."

"McBride, Patterson, pull everyone back to this side," Troy ordered. "Move it!" Again there was no need for the order to be relayed. "Bring it on, Mean Machine."

Sergeant Meenachan directed the next barrage fifty meters closer. With the first volley the ground shook and I could hear the explosions, see the smoke. As the shells came closer, though, I near choked on the sickening smell of war. " . . . three guns, two volleys, same target. Over." He asked Lieutenant Troy if he wanted napalm.

"Negative. Bring the H-E in about twenty meters closer, one round at a time, thirty seconds apart, then sporadic for three minutes."

"Done."

The shelling stopped. The odor lingered.

"Radio," Lieutenant Troy yelled. I raced to his side. "Gimlet 5, this is Alpha 1. Over."

"Gimlet 5."

Lieutenant Troy gave his report, including his belief that the enemy we had engaged was a mix of Viet Cong and North Vietnamese Regulars. He told Major Baldwin that our patrol would not pursue them because their route of escape had been expedient, not planned. Rather, he said, we would enter the jungle at the point where the NVRs had come out. He reasoned that they must have come from a base camp in that direction and that is likely where we would find Richardson and Irvin. The XO agreed and said that he would continue to drop harassment H-E rounds near the crash site for two hours, hoping to keep Charley off our backs until we could get deep enough into the jungle to elude them.

"... One more thing, Alpha 1. Verify that you have one interpreter, the senior man, Captain Thuoc. Over."

"Roger that."

"No impact on you, Alpha 1, but junior man turned up missing when Alpha 6 and his men returned to base."

Captain Thuoc sat near enough to monitor the conversation between Lieutenant Troy and Major Hernandez. He became agitated, agitated enough for Troy to break the transmission with HQ, saying he would get back ASAP.

The sight of the younger interpreter as he came screaming out of the jungle just as the fire fight began was a blur I had almost forgotten in the fog of war. "Viet gian. Phuoc is Viet gian," Captain Thuoc said tersely to Lieutenant Troy in a tone somewhere between frustration and deep anger. "He is traitor." Anger. Although the pieces didn't come together right away for me, Troy had total confidence in Thuoc. He told me to get back on the radio right away and tell HQ that we had sighted the junior interpreter and suspected him to be an enemy agent; we would proceed as he had advised earlier.

We had no way of knowing at the time that Phuoc, who had dropped in at the crash site with the first sortie, had slipped unnoticed into the jungle while the squads were setting up their perimeter. He was more than the traitor Captain Thuoc had characterized him. He was a spy. Having attended the BTOC briefing, he knew our entire plan. He knew that the Troy patrol was hidden in the bush, lying in wait to observe enemy activity. He knew our number, our weapon strength, and our mission.

The best guess is that he didn't make it to the NVR base camp in time to warn his comrades until after they had set back out for the clearing.

"Saddle up," Lieutenant Troy ordered. "When we find Phuoc, we'll find Richardson and Irvin."

"Viet gian," Captain Thuoc muttered, shaking his head in a gesture of disgust.

Birth of a Soldier

It will help to know why Lieutenant Troy placed so much trust in Captain Thuoc, for, given the revelation about Phuoc, an attentive reader might also suspect Thuoc as an accomplice to his countryman. Not so. Troy knew his story. As revealed to me much after this episode in the safety of our Chu Lai compound, Captain Thuoc had long fought the various communist leaning military-political factions that arose in Vietnam after the defeat of the French at Dien Bien Phu in 1954.

Thuoc was born in 1915 in Kim Lien, a village in Nghe An Province, an area renowned for its resistance to foreign oppression. Inhabitants were particularly staunch in their opposition to French colonialism. It may also interest the reader to know that this was coincidentally the birthplace of Nguyen Sinh Sac, father of Nguyen Sinh Cung (born in 1890), the man who would come to be known to the world as Ho Chi Minh. From an early age Thuoc rebelled intellectually rather than as an armed militant. He despised French arrogance that sought to demean the Vietnamese people as somehow inferior; he viewed the French intruders as unwelcome and inhumane.

Thuoc embraced, as did Nguyen Sinh Cung before him, the more palatable culture of the Chinese which he learned mainly through studies in Confucianism. A superior student, he achieved the level of tu tai, in effect, a college graduate—very rare in the agrarian society of Vietnam. (Nguyen Sinh Cung attained the next level of formal academic achievement, cu nhan, recommended man.) Thuoc loved language studies, including French and English as well as Chinese, and botany, not unsurprising for someone born in the tropics; but most of all he enjoyed the study of history which he saw as the continual movement of humanity toward individual perfection. As a serious student of history, he understood the role wars played throughout the centuries, on all continents, in all civilizations. Nevertheless, he rejected the idea that wars are inevitable, or even that they are glorious. "War," he would tell his students in the thatched hut schoolhouse back in Kim Lien, "has no victors, only victims. War, my children, is the manifestation of human failure. When each human being in this world finds peace within himself, then the whole world will be at peace." Before dismissal at the end of every school day, Master Thuoc extended his arms laterally several inches from his sides, faced the palms of his hands toward the class, and said reverently, "Peace be with you."

The armistice at the end of World War I did not end all wars, as promised, and likewise the defeat of the French did not bring lasting peace to Vietnam. Instead, separate internal factions positioned themselves to seize power, most tilting toward one form of communism or another. Although Ho Chi Minh himself had quoted from both American and French Declarations of Independence in a speech in 1945, his use of words like democracy and equality had little correlation to their Western derivatives. Master Thuoc—student, educated man, teacher, pacifist—did not fit; in fact, he refused to align himself with any of the parties in search of power.

One day in 1955 a former student, Nguyen Cao Dai, now an ardent member of Mat tran To quoc, the Fatherland Front, visited his former teacher at the schoolhouse in Kim Lien. Arriving just before closing, he stood near the entryway and watched Master Thuoc release his charges with his traditional "Peace be with you." The children filed out. Nguyen Cao Dai greeted the Master but showed no deference to him, not bowing, even slightly, as a sign of respect.

"You still preach peace, I see, Master Thuoc."

"Nguyen Cao Dai, it is my pleasure to see you again. Peace is my deepest hope for our people. You know that."

"Yes, Master Thuoc," he replied, "but peace demands struggle. You above all should know that. We have rid ourselves of the blood-sucking French" (Thuoc began to cringe inside at the language he never taught and the tone he had never heard from his pupil) "and today, today Master Thuoc, Mat tran To quoc struggles to drive all foreigners from our land. That is the only road to the peace you and I desire."

"Ah, yes, Nguyen Cao Dai, I know well the teachings of Nguyen Sinh Cung and your party's program of land reform." Thuoc paused and touched his index finger to his lip, assuming—trying to assume—the demeanor of teacher once again. "But tell me, shall we cleanse our sacred land of all foreigners?"

"Yes."

"And the Chinese, Nguyen Cao Dai, shall Mat tran To quoc ask Chinese soldiers and Chinese political advisors, and . . ."

"You know very well, Master Thuoc, that the Chinese and Vietnamese are brothers." Nguyen was losing patience. "Did I not learn about Confucius from you yourself?"

"Yes . . ."

Nguyen Cao Dai's authoritative posture and tone of voice effectively reversed their prior roles. "And was it not from you yourself, Master Thuoc, that I learned to despise colonialism and imperialism and to love our Fatherland?"

Thuoc could no longer look at his inquisitor. His eyes fixed at a platoon of purposeful ants marching along the dirt floor toward the exit. "That love is in all of us. I merely showed you that it was there."

"I was sent here, Master Thuoc, to ask you to join us."

"To join Mat tran To quoc? You know that I cannot. I cannot . . ."

Impatient interruption: "The struggle for absolute freedom has begun, Mister Thuoc." Nguyen Cao Dai's use of this less accommodating form of address stung Thuoc. "If you are not with us, you are against us. I ask you once again, will you join us?"

"History tells us . . ." Thuoc began bravely, although he was afraid.

"I am not interested in history. I am not interested in your stories of Greece and Rome, of Ming and Samurai. They are fairy tales. All history is fairy tale. Today, Mister Thuoc, what we do today is all that matters for what will become of us tomorrow. Will you join us?"

"I wish you well, Nguyen Cao Dai," Thuoc said, finding the courage to look directly at the younger man. "But I can be of no use to you."

"You will regret this decision, Mister Thuoc."

There was tragic truth to this threat. Thuoc Van Li regretted for the rest of his life that he had ever met Nguyen Cao Dai.

The next morning, shortly after the school day had begun, Nguyen Cao Dai appeared again at the schoolhouse door. In a controlled, icy voice he told the children to go outside and sit near the flower garden which he knew Master Thuoc cultivated for many years with tender pride. "Do as he says, children," Master Thuoc said calmly, although he himself began to tremble.

"Mister Thuoc," Nguyen Cao Dai said, using the same icy monotone with which he had told the children to leave, "today you are by your own choice an enemy of the Fatherland Front.

My comrades and I conclude, however, that in the future you may prove useful to our cause." Thuoc shook uncontrollably. "Today you begin your journey toward enlightenment. Come with me."

Outside the Palace of Knowledge, as Master Thuoc often referred to his schoolhouse, the children had gathered nervously near the flower garden with the smiling Buddha. Shock overcame him. The first person he saw was his delicate wife Thuy who was held at each arm by men who had been born in Kim Lien—Thuoc knew them as children—but had migrated north to escape the French, eventually to fight and defeat them. The anguish that distorted Thuy's face obliterated the natural beauty of her five-month-old pregnancy. Another man standing near Thuy held a scythe the farmers used to reap their rice. He stepped forward.

"No," Thuoc yelled. "I will join."

Thuy struggled uselessly. "Husband, dear husband," she cried. She howled, "What have I done?"

Thuoc tried to run to his wife but was caught immediately by two men, very young men, who had been standing closely behind him and Nguyen Cao Dai. "I will join." Confused and frightened, the children wept. Buddha stared.

"Yes, Mr. Thuoc, you will join the Fatherland Front some day. Today you are not worthy. Today you and your students will learn that the glorious future of Vietnam will not be delayed by the stupidity of one misinformed man."

"No. No," Thuy screeched, struggling to loose herself from her guards.

"Mama!" A boy of six ran from the garden with arms outstretched to reach and touch his mother. The man with the scythe lunged and, with the skill of a craftsman at one with the tool of his trade, cocked his arms to the side and swung mightily. The curve of the blade ripped through the child's neck. Blood spewed onto the blouse covering Thuy's swollen belly. His head bounced off his fallen torso and rolled to the ground at her feet.

Thuy fainted. Thuoc collapsed. The children cried out in horror, too stunned to look away, too frightened to run. The man on Thuoc's left grabbed a fistful of his hair and jerked his head back so that he could not avoid the unthinkable, unbearable scene. The cutthroat started toward Thuoc . . .

"My son. My son. Oh, Thuy," he cried.

. . . spun himself in the opposite direction and paused as if to say, "It's over."

"Thuy. Beautiful, darling Thuy."

The butcher inhaled deeply. He swung the scythe above his right shoulder and hacked at Thuy's inanimate body. He struck again. And again. And again until he tired from berserk blood rage. Thuy's dismembered body lay scattered on the ground, flies gathering like vultures. In an afterthought of me too complicity one of Thuy's captors trampled a flower bed and pushed the Buddha face first to the hallowed ground.

And that is how this man of peace learned about pure evil. That day he became a soldier.

"Captain Thuoc, do you have any idea where Phuoc may have fled," Captain Troy asked.

"No, Captain Troy." He looked older. His eyelids were heavy, his face wrinkled, his shoulders slumped. "No." Captain Thuoc went on to tell Lieutenant Troy that Phuoc lived in Chu Lai "before Americans came. No family."

"No family," Troy repeated, "and no country."

"Yes, Lieutenant. A traitor has no country."

The patrol filed into the jungle where Phuoc Viet gian had vanished.

Chapter 12
Abandon All Hope

"To give light to them that sit in darkness and in the shadow of death, to guide our feet into the way of peace."
Luke, 1:79

A guard untied the lashes at two corners of the top side of Lieutenant Richardson's cage and swung it open. "Get out," Major Phuoc Ai Quoc ordered. He did. The tiger cages lay next to the pit Richardson dug the night before. The major closed the lid. "Sit."

Hardly able to stand, Richardson found it equally difficult to sit on the tiger cage because he ached all over: from his wounds, from forced labor, from the dents along his body wherever it came to rest against the bamboo, from fatigue. Don't lose your honor, he insisted to himself. "And Specialist Irvin, Major. What about him?"

"Your friend Irvin, Mister Richardson, is a burden we will soon be rid of." He then said something to Point Man who removed the top section of Irvin's cage then rotated it so that the top was now the side. Irvin tumbled inside like a raggedy blanket in a clothes dryer. The keeper tilted the cage and shook Irvin out. "There is your friend Irvin, Mister Richardson."

"Will you give him a drink of water? Please." Richardson justified this plea for mercy from his enemy because he made it not for himself.

"That would be foolish," the major replied matter of factly. "I will not waste precious water on an American coward." He said something to one of his henchmen who handed him a canteen. The major unscrewed the top and took a long swig. "Ah," he sighed, water dripping down his chin. He offered the canteen to Richardson who reached for it with his left hand. The major pulled it back. He and the guards laughed.

"Dog Richardson, it is time for you to tell me what you know. I want to know where the other two war criminals fled."

Richardson's voice was weak and raspy as sand. And just as dry. Maintain your honor. "I don't know."

The major snapped his fingers. The Pervert, who appeared too young to be drafted into the United States Army, stepped to within six feet in front of Lieutenant Richardson, raised his rifle to his shoulder, and aimed point blank at his head. "Where did you order them to go?"

"I gave no order. I do not know where they went."

"You will answer my question, Richardson, Paul, First Lieutenant, United States Army." He gave an order.

. . . I forgive those who trespass against me. . . .

The firing squad of one turned forty-five degrees to his right and lowered his aim until the barrel pointed straight at Irvin. "Last time. Where?"

"Chu Lai," Richardson said immediately to save Irvin's life. He fully expected Major Phuoc to force him to fulfill his, Phuoc's, prophecy, "You 'will' tell me what I want to know." In anticipation of that dread moment Prisoner of War Richardson had rehearsed the false answer, Chu Lai. He knew that the actual answer to Phuoc's repeated question had little if any military value. The purpose of the inquisition had nothing at all to do with a search for truth. It had everything to do with one person acknowledging to another orally—publicly—the hopelessness of his situation, no matter how just his cause or righteous his stand. In order to save his life, the defeated must say—say out loud, that's the key—say that his conqueror is right. This always means that he must lie. He must say exactly the opposite of what he believes, admit to a hostile audience that survival, under any condition, is more important than dying for truth.

Paul Richardson, like any of us, had no way of knowing his physical limits. He dreaded the torture he fully expected so much that the thought of it made him nauseous. In an attempt to separate anguished mind from wracked body during his grave digging ordeal he forced himself to formulate bogus answers to anticipated questions. And since The Voice had harped so much on where Sullivan and Nash had headed, he wanted most of all to be able to lie convincingly when his body surrendered to pain. Honor. Chu Lai was the plausible misdirection because it was in fact an American base camp, even though it was much farther from the crash site than Fire Base Bravo. With virtually every handfull of dirt he managed to pile outside the pit he had repeated to himself the words Chu Lai. At first he would imagine the question as he was scooping dirt into his hands, Where are they? At the release of the dirt he'd reply, Chu Lai. As he grew weaker and more fatigued the simple three-word question shrunk to one, Where?

One side of his mind asked a thousand times, Where are they? A thousand times the other side answered, Chu Lai. The next thousand times it asked, Where? Another thousand times the reply was still Chu Lai. Weaker and weaker, the question mattered so little that he actually forgot it; Chu Lai were the only words extant in his consciousness. Chu Lai, huff puff. Chu Lai, huff puff. If The Voice had asked, Where were you born, he would have said, Chu Lai. If The Voice asked, What is your mother's maiden name, he would say Chu Lai. Who won the 1965 World Series? Chu Lai. He had effectively washed his brain of all proper nouns other than Chu Lai.

When Richardson answered the ultimatum with "Chu Lai," Phuoc said, "That is better, Lieutenant Richardson. I told you that you would tell me what I want to know." Major Phuoc offered the canteen again. Richardson took it and drank lustily, almost gagging on his swollen tongue. The rifleman lowered his weapon. Gulp. "But you did not tell me the truth, Dog Richardson. For that, you will suffer." Gulp. Major Phuoc issued an order. Pervert raised the carbine hip high and shot three bullets into Irvin. Bang, bang, bang. Richardson felt each round rifle through his own heart. He wept.

The major turned away from Richardson as though in disgust. He barked an order and pointed into the jungle. Four of his men disappeared. Richardson stared morosely at Irvin's corpse, unable to forgive himself for the death he could not prevent.

The band of four returned. First two appeared carrying a body slung between them on a bamboo pole. The second pair bore a similar load. They dropped their bounty next to Irvin. Richardson started at the sight. No one restrained him from going to inspect. Sully and Nash had not made it to Fire Base Bravo. Their clothes were torn, their faces badly bruised. Richardson retched when he noticed on closer examination that Sullivan's ears were missing. Did it matter? He was dead. Yes, it mattered.

Nash? Is he dead?

"This, Dog Richardson, is the proof of your lies."

Nash, barely alive, tried to open his swollen eyes at the sound of The Voice. He could not. Richardson stroked Nash's blood-matted hair, again with no restraint from his captors. "What have they done?" Spec-4 Nash recognized Lieutenant Richardson's voice.

"Sir? Lieutenant Richardson? Is that you," he slurred through broken teeth. I can't see. I can't . . ."

"Yes, Andy, yes. It's me. You're going to be all right." He lied again.

"Lieutenant Sullivan . . . Sir . . . they . . . they . . . I . . . I . . ."

"I know, Andy. I know."

Major Phuoc allowed the dismal reunion to go on for a while, actually until Nash lapsed into merciful sleep, his head at rest on Richardson's thigh. "One of my other glorious units captured your friends at the ARVN camp you call Fire Base Bravo. After they killed all Vietnamese traitors who did not run like mice, these two were interrogated." The Voice began to pace professorially as before. "Your copilot and machine gunner were not trying to flee to Chu Lai, Dog Richardson. Their destination was Fire Base Bravo." As he said Bravo, he bent low and smashed the back of his clenched fist into Richardson's face. "You lied." Blood trickled from one nostril of the broken nose.

"Lieutenant Sullivan was very helpful." The Voice turned lecturer again. "Not right away." He informed Richardson that his unit commander spoke enough English to extract more than name rank and serial number from Sullivan and Nash. Richardson tried not to picture the scene of horror at the fire base . . . to no use. The sound of Sully's screams as the blade ripped down the side of his head and cheek pierced his ear drums. He closed his eyes tightly. The lecture went on . . . and on.

"I do not know precisely how this dog died, Mister Richardson. Slowly and with much pain, I am sure. We are very good at such things." His voice was without emotion. "The pain you yourself feel now is the scratch of a mosquito. The bite of the crocodile awaits." He walked to where several of his men were sitting, eating rice they had cooked over a small fire. A few moments later Silent One brought a wooden bowl, half-filled with rice and indistinguishable chunks of something Richardson would rather not know, and placed it next to him.

Nurse Richardson reached for the bowl, trying not to disturb his patient. He brought it near Nash's mouth, close enough that the smell caused Nash to stir. "Where . . . what . . . hmph," he mumbled, still unable to open his eyes.

"It's okay, Andy. I've got something for you to eat." Richardson picked at the rice and placed a few grains at Nash's lips. Nash's tongue came out slowly and licked the Good Samaritan's soiled fingers. Another dose. Nash couldn't get enough. He darted his head forward and sucked the tips of Richardson's fingers into his mouth. "Easy. Easy. There's more." Richardson gave himself two small portions and fed the rest to Nash.

All the while, Silent One and Pervert were digging a hole with spades on the other side of the camp, just inside the wood line. Two others dragged the fly-infested corpses to what would become their unmarked grave. When they deemed it deep enough, the diggers swept Sullivan and Irvin with their feet into the hole. Pervert lingered, fumbling ghoulishly under the body parts before raking the dirt into a mound.

Into the Dark of Night

Lieutenant Troy's posse stopped and dropped instantly in unison at the sound of the three shots in the distance that had sent Irvin to Kingdom Come, each man pointing toward the cracks like golden retrievers. The Ranger took out his compass to shoot an azimuth; Eddie the woodsman did the same. The patrol headed off stealthily in single file behind Tommy who without waiting for an order assumed point. The squad had done this before. Eddie guided Tommy with hand signals along a direct line of intermediate landmarks in the dark jungle—tree trunks, saplings, anything that stood between us and the knell of the rifle.

Pucker. My body wanted to sprint at the pace of my racing pulse. My brain called back the ambush that had claimed Jake's life. I swung my head instinctively over my shoulder expecting to see a bad guy, maybe more, ready to open up on us, momentarily stunned by the flashback of Jake's obscene death. Nothing there. Fact is, I couldn't see anything past Lieutenant Troy's silhouette. "Keep it tight, Brother," he whispered. "Nobody behind us."

Troy or someone may have known how far away the shots were fired. I sure didn't. But for sure we now had a defined destination, and getting there undetected in the dead of night was all that mattered.

If I told you how long it took us to reach the deserted base camp, I'd be lying. No clue. All I remember is how carefully I took each step—ball of the foot first, outside edge, then heel, in order to minimize noise—and staring at the FO in front of me in dire fear of getting separated. He'd duck under a branch, I'd do the same. He'd hold one aside so that it wouldn't snap back into the place Nature intended until I could grasp it and wait for Troy to accept the handoff. Tommy and Eddie, muted pied pipers, led our mime troupe.

We stopped. I think I froze. When Troy touched my arm, my bones jumped but I didn't move a muscle. He put a finger to his lips and passed me. In a few seconds we were moving again. Shortly, I saw Eddie and Tommy laying prone on either side of Troy, weapons aimed into the moonlight-striped clearing. Troy was kneeling with his back to it, directing the rest of us alternately to one side and then the other. "Two meters past the last man, then down."

I couldn't figure whether we were on offense or defense. After what seemed a long time word from Troy passed down the line that we were there for the night. "Every other man awake. When you get drowsy, poke your brother." Meenachan whispered that he'd take first watch. "Just close your eyes, Nick. I'll wake you in an hour." Sleep? Who's kidding who here? But sleep I did. Time, however, had no meaning, so I don't know whether it was one hour or five before Meenachan roused me. Nor do I have any idea how long I stayed on watch, but however long it was lasted until dawn. The morning sun allowed me to see that everyone was now alert.

Troy and Smith huddled and then duck walked in opposite directions. Sergeant Smith came my way and whispered, "Stay down," as he passed. The two highest ranking men on the patrol skimmed the woodline and met at the other side of the abandoned camp. I had come a long, long way from the training exercises at what I can only characterize now as Fantasy Land, Fort Polk. Real soldiers don't need Sir Sergeant martinets to motivate them; sometimes—often, in fact—we act without orders at all, like Tommy taking point. Real leaders don't treat their men as sorry excuses of something. They treat us with respect, thereby earning ours. And in the case of present circumstances, because they share the danger of their subordinates, real leaders make on the spot decisions that will likely affect the lives of all, their own included.

Lieutenant Troy and Sergeant Smith, silent partners, performed a *danse macabre* to a captivated audience. They spoke briefly to each other, then Smith, walking nearly upright just inside the tree line, came back to us. "No booby traps," he said. "But be careful. We may have missed 'em."

I had this eerie feeling about the place. The teams fanned out slowly and each man went as if to a pre-designated spot. "Over here, Nick. Sergeant Meenachan, you too," Troy said. He told me to get on the air and establish contact with BTOC.

The task distracted me from the peculiar mix of unfamiliar smells that made me queasy.

Troy and his FO knelt over Meenachan's map. "Yes, Sir, I have a good idea where we are. But I'd like to confirm."

"Suggestion?"

Meenachan pointed to an intersecting road and river. "I'm pretty sure we're less than a click from Fire Base Bravo." He asked Troy to give him a rifleman. "We'll get a visual."

"Let me think about it for a minute." Troy called to Smith and the two of them began scanning the open ground. "Three shells over here, Sarge. We're in the right place." He told me to tell BTOC to stand by "just a minute."

"Over here, Calloway." Sergeant Smith was on his knees scraping at a mound of fresh dirt. "Don't know what Charlie had for dinner last night, but it stinks." I wasn't anxious to help him dig for I didn't know what: garbage maybe, or worse, a latrine? "Ah, Sweet Jesus," he said slowly, collapsing so that his hamstrings covered his heels. He removed his helmet with his soiled fingers. "No."

Lieutenant Troy came to the graveside. I took the radio off my back and started removing dirt with my bare hands, not really wanting to go any deeper, not able to stop. Troy reached for the microphone. "Gimlet 6. Alpha 6. Over."

"Go, Alpha 6."

Troy reported our discovery. "We'll exhume the bodies and return to LZ for dustoff. Make sure it's not hot." Major Baldwin rogered, not offended by Troy's authoritarian tone. "Something bugging me, though," Troy said to no one in particular after signing off. "Why bother to bury the bodies?"

It took an eternity to uncover them. I had trouble seeing through tear swelled eyes. "No. No, don't lift them out. They could be booby trapped." Smith's words sounded callous at the time.

"They're already dead."

"And you will be too."

I couldn't finish the job. Captain Thuoc touched my shoulder. "You be all right, GI." He knelt at the grave and probed beneath the corpses with his hands. I couldn't watch. I had seen too much death already. It wasn't that long ago my parents had protected me from the peaceful sight of Grandma laid out for eternal rest in her cushioned casket. In a minute or two Captain Thuoc raised himself to his feet, clutching a pinless hand grenade. Lieutenant Troy rolled his handkerchief into a rope and wrapped it around the mini-bomb to prevent the handle from flying loose thereby triggering it. "Thank you, Captain," he said.

Our Vietnamese brother gently dragged the wretched bodies from the hole. I stared at them, unable to look away. The sight of the meandering parade of overfed, blood-stained insects and the stench of rotting human flesh repelled me. Flies appeared. Where do they come from? I was about to be sick.

"Dhhown. Dhhown," McBride cried loud enough for us to hear, trying not to give us away. I fell to my side, then rolled onto my stomach and reached for my weapon. Lieutenant Troy and Sergeant Smith low crawled to either side of the Bravo Team leader. M-16 safety switches clicked to Off. Or was it the sound of twigs cracking under the weight of human feet? Having propped my left elbow in front of my face, now cradling the plastic stock of my rifle in my left hand and staring down the barrel past the sight, I saw indistinguishable movement. I felt naked. Sergeant Meenachan and I lay vulnerable in the clearing. We dare not move. We're dead men. Maybe they won't see us. Schwish-crack-schwish-crack. Pucker.

Oh, my God, I am heartily sorry for having offended Thee . .

.

Here They Come Again

Schwish-crack-schwish-crack.

... I firmly resolve to amend my life ...

Captain Thuoc rose and walked toward the sound.

"Dhhown. Get down."

Thuoc ignored Troy's warning. He walked a half-dozen paces. He stopped. The sound of alien footsteps went silent. Facing away from us, the enigmatic man of two tongues spoke calmly in Vietnamese. A weak male voice responded. I couldn't see its owner. Thuoc gestured into the jungle as if to say, "Come, follow me," as he turned back toward us. "This is not the enemy," he told Lieutenant Troy, his expressionless face adding veracity to his words as he crossed back inside our circle.

I bored in on an unarmed figure following him, and then another, smaller. Much smaller. Huh? Is this some kind of crazy dream? I had drawn a bead on the old man and little boy we saw at the crash site. My barrel sight searched for another. Nothing. I pointed slightly away, although still running on high-test adrenaline.

Captain Thuoc introduced Lieutenant Troy to Mister Van Tran, after conferring a few moments with him, ". . . and his grandson, Cao Tran." The old man bowed respectfully to the officer. Probably because of his confidence in Captain Thuoc, Troy returned the greeting, bowing to him with equal depth. Cao tried his best to hide behind his grandfather.

The three Vietnamese squatted at the side of camp opposite the grave site. Thuoc patted the little boy's hand at one point, the hand that clung tightly to his grandfather's shirt. He pointed toward the bodies. The old man looked, closed his eyes, and made what appeared to be the Catholic sign of the cross. The little boy took a sidelong glance at the pitiful sight then buried his face in his grandfather's shirt. He showed himself peek-a-boo fashion.

It was the first time I actually saw the boy's face. Although I looked straight at him, however, I couldn't pick out his features because I found myself transfixed by the isosceles triangular pit that began at the base of his nose and ran down to his mouth, leaving his crooked front teeth exposed. I tried to imagine what horrible thing caused this mutilation.

I know now that the boy was born with a cleft palate left uncorrected by the routine surgery that easily corrects the condition in American newborns. All I ever knew before about birth defects was Frankie Maquire who wasn't allowed to take gym in grammar school because, Mom said, poor soul, he was born with a bad heart. He always looked fine to me. Mom often asked me if anybody at school was picking on that nice boy Frankie whose sainted mother had to work two jobs to keep up with her son's doctor bills. "Don't you let anybody tease Frankie. You hear, Nicky?" I had trouble associating any woman who didn't dress like the Blessed Virgin with canonization. Lots of people in the project worked two jobs. And Mr. Maguire, by the way, seemed to have enough money to spend most evenings at the Dew Drop Inn. Sometimes he didn't bother making it home after work to eat his sainted wife's cooking. Kids don't connect all those scattered biographical dots until later in life. The Maguires moved away before sixth grade and I didn't give any more thought about kids with problems. Until now.

Five minutes passed, maybe ten, before Thuoc came over to Troy who was now sitting near me and Sergeant Meenachan. "Mister Tran come this way every day with little boy," he said. "When he know soldiers here, he bring rice to them, and tea."

I'm thinking that Troy's thinking the same thing I'm thinking: this guy's VC, or at least a VC sympathizer. He just admitted it, didn't he? Should I be afraid of him? Are we going to take him prisoner? Did anyone at least frisk this guy? What the heck are we going to do with the kid?

"Did he tell you where these soldiers went, Captain Thuoc."

"Yes, Lieutenant. They go to Mister Tran's village, close by Bravo Base."

The whole thing confused me. If the old man is VC, why would he rat on his pals so easily? Doesn't make sense. Is the little boy dangerous? If Troy was thinking what I was thinking, he didn't show it. He told Thuoc to bring Mr. Tran to where we were sitting. Cao trailed along, still attached to his grandfather's garment.

Through a patient series of "Ask him this" and "Ask him thats," Troy got the old man to tell him everything he wanted to know. Not only did the VC control Mr. Tran's village, they had also infiltrated the ARVN company at Fire Base Bravo. The place we were now at served as a rendezvous for VC and North Vietnamese soldiers as well as a staging area for their guerrilla operations.

"Are you sure this man is not our enemy, Captain?"

Thuoc did not translate Troy's question. Rather, he answered it himself. "No, Lieutenant. Do not make wrong conclusion from, how you say, circumstantial evidence. He is not enemy because he bring soldiers food. He bring food because he is too old for them to make him fight." He paused. "This man like many of my countrymen. Whoever win the war make no difference to him. VC tell him bring food, he bring food. No choice."

Lieutenant Troy asked Captain Thuoc if he thought he could convince Mr. Tran to show us the best way to Fire Base Bravo—tilting his head graciously toward the old man as he said his name. "I tell him already, Lieutenant, that you are honorable man, and he is not prisoner."

"Good, I guess."

"I tell him he and Cao free to go home." Thuoc smiled one of those I know something you don't know smiles. "I tell him we going same way."

Chapter 13
The Bigger Picture

> "No man is an Island,
> entire of it self;
> every man is . . .
> a part of the main . . ."
> "Meditation XVII," John Donne

I can report to you now some of the things I didn't know then. It will come as no surprise, I am sure, that, considering the events of the past two days, my new world actually had shrunk even more than Lieutenant Troy proclaimed an eon ago in the Chu Lai mess. Not only was I unaware of anything happening beyond this mini-world that wasn't New Jersey or Timbuktu, I didn't care. I truly did not care about anything but the immediate present. Searching for two GIs, finding two corpses, and having to place unconditional trust in the untested good faith of a war weary old man who brings his grandson to feed the enemy can do that to a guy. Life in a combat zone, I discovered, is primordial not magnanimous, insular not visionary. But there were in fact important things happening beyond my semi-private here and now.

Permit me a convoluted, metaphoric attempt at explanation. My PRC-25 was our umbilical cord to Mother BTOC. Although to characterize our patrol as a babe toddling through the woods might seem trite, it works to some extent. In her protectorate role, for example, Mother had smothered enemy predators with artillery yesterday to give us breathing space. We—and her other offspring operating in the area—fed her information; she digested it, later to decide how best to act on it ... or not. I wasn't thinking quite this poetically at the time, mind you. At the time, I worried mostly about how I, how we, would get ourselves out of there. Being my brother's keeper had sadly slipped back in my consciousness. Fortunately, the brothers in Mother's bunker, the brain center, were working round the clock plotting ways to bring us home.

Here's what they knew, and here's how they planned to help us get back to the hearth.

You already know what Troy reported at the crash site, including the sighting and confirmation that the interpreter Phuoc had betrayed us. Before we set out for Fire Base Bravo with our newfound guides, Lieutenant Troy briefed Major Baldwin about our approximate location and intent to head directly toward the camp. When he reported the deaths of Lieutenant Sullivan and Specialist Irvin, the XO asked for clarification: "You mean Richardson and Irvin. Correct? Confirm."

"Negative. Sully's dead. No sign of Paul. We covered the bodies and will retrieve them when the original mission is complete. Now looking for Richardson and Nash." Baldwin could not, did not doubt the accuracy of the Ranger's identification of the bodies. But there was also no doubt that the original transmission from the ARVN camp known as Fire Base Bravo identified the aviator and gunner as "Sullivan" and Nash. The XO sent for Colonel Hernandez.

The BTOC staff struggled to make sense of the disparate information they had. Major Baldwin drew a triangle on their wall map with a grease pencil hoping somehow to see a connection. As he gathered his thoughts, Colonel Hernandez came in. There were the remains of the helicopter at a site that Major Baldwin now identified as Point Alpha; there was the incommunicado ARVN camp at Fire Base Bravo which he renamed

Point Bravo; and there was Point Charlie, the jungle abyss where we found Sullivan and Irvin and placed our trust in Tran and Cao. When Baldwin in effect blessed Troy's plan to go to Bravo in search of Richardson and Nash, he assured him that we would have support when we got there. He offered no specifics.

Colonel Hernandez took charge. "Major," he said, "report, please."

Baldwin first expressed concern for the lack of knowledge about the enemy's size and capabilities. Gimlet 6 then let his second in command summarize aloud what they all knew so that there was no confusion. One, the bad guys had plucked a whirlybird from the night sky; two, they killed at least two GIs; three, they transposed Sullivan's body for Richardson's somewhere between Points Bravo and Charley; and number four, they infiltrated the BTOC sanctuary in the person of Mr. Phuoc.

"The enemy is well informed and well armed, Gentlemen," Colonel Hernandez said, "and he is lethal. We're going to get Troy big time help on the ground." He dismissed Baldwin's suggestion to "soften up" the fire base with an artillery barrage. He had already formulated his plan. He approached the map.

"The 12th Cav has been operating here—mostly recon stuff," he said, making small circles with the pointer in a region northeast of Point Bravo." Major Baldwin, tell them to deploy a tank squadron, or whatever they can spare, down to the fire base."

"Yes, Sir."

"Tell them to set up a line on the back side of the camp— here—and behind this village. They are to assume that any Vietnamese man, woman, or child coming toward them is the enemy."

"Rules of engagement?" the XO asked.

They were simple. "If threatened, shoot to kill."

Chapter 14
East of Eden

> "The voice of thy brother's blood
> crieth unto me from the ground."
> Genesis, 4:10

Fire Base Bravo—just a defoliated mound with triple canopy jungle 50 meters to the south and west, a patch of rice paddies edging it on the north, doglegging east, and a dozen or so hootches crowding the banks of a narrow river on the east—had morphed from artillery-protected compound to graveyard. American soldiers and their ARVN counterparts, not counting those who were actually Viet Cong infiltrators of course, had little to fear from their docile rice farming neighbors. All who were left to do the work of centuries were women and children, very old men, and a few young men, physically handicapped by or from God knows what. Maybe their missing limbs were absent at birth. Maybe polio claimed them, or plague. Maybe these broken men were purple-hearted veterans of war against the French or the Americans or their brothers from either side of the DMZ. It didn't really matter. Now they tended rice and dug graves.

They took little notice when Major Phuoc and his marauders arrived. A few, including a soldier-age, one-legged man with bamboo crutches, inspected the unconscious body of Lieutenant Richardson, curious if he was alive or dead. Alive, barely. No shirt. No boots. Stripes of cruelty crisscrossing his torso and limbs. Better he were dead they thought but would not say. Pervert approached.

"Murderer, Seng," he said to his brother, spitting on his prey. "Where is Cao?"

"Your son and Uncle Van left along their usual route to meet you at the spot. How did you not meet them?"

"We returned along the river bank for speed," Pervert said. "Americans will be here soon. We are sure of that."

"Seng Tran," it was the voice of Major Phuoc, "you will cut the ears off this dog."

"Yes."

"We will show these imperialists once again that their cause is hopeless. They must be punished."

Seng Tran stood in emotionless silence. Pervert grabbed Lieutenant Richardson by his ears, pulled his head up as far as the spine would allow, then dropped it face first into the dirt.

The Voice: "Remember, Seng Tran, when you perform the small duties you are still able to carry out for the fatherland you also avenge yourself. Think of this invader as the Frenchman that stole your manhood. Remember that, Seng Tran. Remember that."

The women, knowing what was expected of them, boiled pots of rice and fish. Their daughters served the soldiers, some not much older than themselves, keeping their eyes toward the ground, trying not to engage the "men" they had come to fear as much as they had come to fear the Americans.

"More," one demanded. And there was more.

"Beer," ordered another. Then another and another.

"Beer," The Voice commanded. "Give my patriots beer."

It seems ridiculous, I know, that anyone might expect a store of beer in this shanty town where water was drawn from the river daily and boiled to render it potable. But even though the word capitalism was an obscenity to ideologues like Major

Phuoc, the marketing concept of finding a need and filling it for a price is universal. And so there was beer.

On those sporadic occasions when helicopters dropped supplies of ammunition and rations into Fire Base Bravo, sometimes missing and hitting the rice paddies, they also occasionally dropped in a supply of American beer. It never seemed enough for the Americans, the locals observed. They filled the niche.

As in all socialist economies, manufacture, distribution, and sale of most consumer goods, including tobacco and alcohol, are state controlled enterprises. No competition. No price wars. No choice. The national beer of Vietnam was Ba Mui Ba, which translates to "33 Beer," brand name origin unknown. It was bottled. One size. Flat. American soldiers were warned not to drink Ba Mui Ba in case those devious commies had slipped crushed glass or poison or some other noxious substance into the bottles before they were capped. But beer is beer, and the so many GIs who weren't old enough to drink legally in the States would, in that tenuous, shrunken world at war, drink whatever and as much as they could get. The villagers got it for them. Everyone was happy: soldiers consumed more alcohol than HQ had allotted or needed to know about, peasants pocketed piasters they might some day be able to buy something with.

Were the soldiers at Fire Base Bravo, at least some of them, drinking the day they were overrun? Does it matter now?

Major Phuoc did not drink. He conceded to allow his soldiers this particular diversion, though, even the young ones, as a kind of conscience cleansing they had come to expect. But the Americans were coming, for sure, and he had that one important piece of business to attend to before disappearing into the jungle to fight another day. Without needing to be told,

Pervert had planted the pole Lieutenant Richardson's blood-raw wrists were still tied behind into the mud at the river bank. He banged it deeper into the less fluid earth beneath the mud using the flat of the ax he carried.

Awake, not wholly alert, and despite Pervert's prodding, the pilot could not stand. Frustrated, Pervert hacked off a length of bamboo from the section that extended above Richardson's head. He threw it to the ground then slashed it in two at an angle. Anxious to join in, and probably in a sycophantic gesture to please their magnanimous commander, a pair of Pervert's comrades, each swigging from a beer bottle, came to his aid. One bear hugged Richardson from behind and pulled him into a near standing position. The other removed his rope belt and tied it so tightly around Richardson's waist his rib cage protruded carcass like from his undernourished frame.

Beltless rammed the mouth of his bottle into the helpless victim's mouth and poured what was left down his throat. Richardson gagged. He vomited. The Brothers Grim laughed. They rapped their bottles together so hard in triumphant toast to each other that the bottles broke. In obeisance to an order of some kind from Pervert, Beltless again grabbed Lieutenant Richardson from the rear, keeping him upright. He still held the top end of the broken bottle in his left hand; and so when he squeezed, the jagged end pierced Richardson's right side, just below the fully visible lowest rib.

Armed now with a pair of bamboo daggers, Pervert drove one and then the other through each of Richardson's feet. This cruel ignoramus probably thought the double impalement would force Richardson to stand, anchored to the ground and propped by the pole. Rather, Richardson's left knee jerked violently at the first strike, lifting his foot free of the mud. Beltless struggled to keep him up. The glass dug deeper. When Pervert struck the stake into his right foot, Richardson dropped to a contorted sitting position, his full weight too much for Beltless to bear. Whatever life remained within him released itself in the loudest cry of pain he had expelled during the ordeal of his captivity. The fresh blood trickling from his side wound mingled with the muddy water.

The villagers had gathered at the river. All of them. No choice.

"This beast is our enemy," Major Phuoc declared. "We have stripped him of his name and military rank because we do not consider him soldier or man." Pervert moved to Lieutenant Paul Richardson, United States Army. He grabbed him by the hair and pulled his head skyward so all were forced to view his monstrous face. "Seng Tran."

Seng Tran hobbled forward using but one crutch. He clutched a knife in his right hand. When he stooped directly in front of the vermin he would butcher, he did not look at his brother, he whom we have come to know only as Pervert. Seng Tran planted his crutch firmly into the shallow mud, leaning on it to make sure it would support him. He raised the knife in his knuckle-white right fist, hilt toward his shoulder, tip pointing at Lieutenant Richardson's head. Grinning, Pervert yanked one last time.

Seng Tran and Paul Richardson's eyes locked.

The Voice: "Seng Tran!"

"Forgive me," Seng Tran said to Paul Richardson who blinked then closed his eyes.

Seng Tran kept the knife in its cocked position, lunged to the front and left in a single twist, and with all his weight behind the thrust he plunged his weapon into Pervert's heart and fell on top of him.

Beltless pounced on Seng Tran, stabbing him repeatedly in the back with his broken bottle. His comrade joined in the carnage. Phuoc shot into the air to bring order to the chaos. His soldiers "fell in," ready now to do his bidding.

The villagers scurried to the rice paddies.

Phuoc led his band across the waist-deep river. They disappeared into the jungle on the other side.

Chapter 15

Mission Complete

> "...
> And to make an end is to make a beginning.
> The end is where we start from."
> *Little Gidding*, 5, T.S. Eliot

The Americans hit the ground instinctively at the sound of the rifle shot. Mister Tran, Cao, and Captain Thuoc merely stopped walking. Lieutenant Troy was leading the patrol. Well, actually, grandfather and grandson were at the head of the pack, but the Ranger was right up there with them. The Fighting Irish came next, then me and Thuoc and the FO, then Alpha Team. We could have been making better time if we simply followed our guides single file along the route they knew so well. No way. Troy insisted on flank security to both sides, which meant that one man from each fire team had to cut his way through the virgin growth ten meters or so to our left and right, maintaining eye contact with one of his brothers so as not to get separated. This was textbook procedure against ambush that, unfortunately, not all Americans on patrol in Vietnam followed. Tommy sure was right about Troy: he was as good as there was in the field; and he was not about to gamble our safety for the sake of speed. God, I love this guy.

"Nick!"

"On the way."

"Team leaders, get your men off the path." They had already done so. The Vietnamese squatted.

"Gimlet 5, Gimlet 5. Alpha 6. Over." Troy reported the single shot he knew came from our destination. Having checked with Sergeant Meenachan, he also gave an approximate coordinate of where we were. "Maybe thirty minutes away."

"Proceed with caution," Major Baldwin said. You know I was puckered ever since the shot. What the XO told Troy after that, however, gave me some relief. "Two squadrons of rumblers headed for Foxtrot Bravo Bravo from the northwest right now. They'll be there before you. Platoon of grunts headed toward the river from the east."

"Roger that," Troy said, apparently relieved himself, although not very demonstrative about it.

"Repeat," Baldwin said. "Proceed with caution. You have plenty of help, Alpha 6."

"Wilco. Out."

I don't know how this guy does it. But a half-hour later, practically to the minute, we broke the wood line and arrived at Fire Base Bravo. I didn't know what to expect. I could hardly believe what I saw. The tankers had set up a perimeter around the entire area, guns pointed into the surrounding black areas. The pucker was gone. Baldwin made good on his word. Bless him.

The peasants—that's the only way I could describe them to myself at the time—milled around outside their homes. If their hovels were teepees, this could have been a scene from a Hollywood western, except this wasn't a good guys versus bad guys fiction created on a back lot back in what I had previously thought of as the real world. This was a horrific reality for real people who lived in real deprivation. All the time. No cowboys and Indians. No diversions for them. No relief. Ever.

Officer Somebody called out to Troy, signaling him to bring us deeper into the ironclad womb his tanks had created. We lowered the weapons we had been cradling at the ready for so long and made our way toward the high ground. We stopped in unison to watch Cao, finally disengaged from his grandfather, sprint toward what we all knew had to be his mother. I guess I could claim that exhaustion brought those tears to my eyes. I won't; that would have been the old me. It was the vision of pure, reciprocal love that overwhelmed me. Cao had made it home where he belonged smothered in mother love. She would not release her hug, nor he his, yet she managed to bring him inside their home. A little girl and two women followed.

Grandfather already knew the truth. He and Master Thuoc were kneeling prayerfully beside the corpses of Seng and Chen Tran. Mr. Tran's forehead touched the ground and he wept. Thuoc arranged himself in the lotus position, while the old man stayed prostrate, slapping the ground in grief. The villagers came close. Are they all family? We turned our heads away. These poor people deserved their privacy.

On the hill we found our own horror. Laying 'neath the shade of a poncho stretched out from the side of one of the tanks was the desecrated, listless body of First Lieutenant Paul Richardson.

"Ah, Sweet Mother of God," Troy said. "What have they done?"

The tank squadron commander tried in vain to lead Troy away from this brother we had set out to recover. "No," Troy said with no disrespect. He knelt reverently at Richardson's side and placed his hand gently on the pilot's chest. We joined him, uncovered, heads bowed. These men are my brothers, Lieutenant Richardson. We've been looking for you. And now our prayers have been answered." Richardson blinked.

I didn't think for once of our search and rescue mission as a pilgrimage. Until that moment. The entire journey flashed before me. It had been an act of faith all along.

During the planning session at BTOC I felt proud of myself and proud of my extended family. We were honor bound to bring the fallen home. Failure to do so was inconceivable. And now I felt ashamed of my pride, humbled by my—our—inability to save Lieutenant Richardson from his suffering, unable to prevent Nash's death. Daddy, is this what you wanted to protect me from but could not? I am so sorry for the war memories that have haunted you. How could I have behaved so stupidly? Forgive me.

"Lieutenant Troy, you've been ordered to return to base with Lieutenant Richardson's dustoff chopper" the officer said. "It will be here any minute."

"I'm not going anywhere without my men, Lieutenant Brown."

"A sortie will extract them in about twenty minutes."

"I'll wait."

A pair of gunships circled the area and a huey with sidecar landed on the fire base. Two medics rushed out and a tanker sergeant directed them to Lieutenant Richardson. Then Colonel Hernandez appeared. What's he doing here? Seeing the battalion commander, Troy walked out to meet him. They shook hands and stopped in private conversation.

"No," we all heard the Ranger cry as he threw his weapon to the ground.

After all we'd been through in the cause of duty and honor, was Lieutenant Troy defying an order from the colonel? Couldn't be. "Get on the chopper," Sergeant Smith muttered as we all stood in disbelief. Troy waved Smith over to the meeting, told him to take charge of the squad, and boarded the helicopter with Colonel Hernandez. The medics secured their patient in the stretcher rigged to the chopper's landing runners and climbed aboard themselves. The ambulance ship lifted off and they were gone.

"What was that all about," anyone could have asked but didn't.

"The lieutenant's son died last night," Sergeant Smith told us.

"Hey, Calloway, is that you?" I turned toward the vaguely familiar voice coming toward me from the river. "Nicky, it's me, Cox."

Although I can't remember what we said to each other during our warm and lingering hand shake, I do remember what happened next. He put his arm around my shoulder and invited me to his tank. "Call your boys," he said. They heard. "Looks like you guys could use a cold beer." Adam Cox's tank carried two coolers, one filled with beer, the other soda. On ice! Beer sounded good. We all reached, instead, for a soda. I guess no one felt much like partying just then. I know I didn't. Whatever my brothers were thinking individually, we all knew that Cox and his tankers had dropped whatever they were doing to answer the call to get us out of hell.

"Maybe later," he said, "we can treat you guys to a golden minute."

"A what?"

"A golden minute. That's when we spray the jungle with our .50-caliber machine guns. If we don't actually hit any Charleys out there, it scares them to death. Can't do it now, though. We've got orders not to shoot 'cause there's more of you ground pounders coming this way." Now I'm back to, do I love this guy or hate him? One thing for sure: I was glad to see him.

"Yo, Cox, get up on your gun," a Spec-4 yelled from the tank to our left. "There's movement out there. The rest of you guys take cover." Things got serious again real quick, but we weren't about to have someone else do our fighting. Our fire teams positioned themselves on line to either side of Cox's cold drink wagon taking aim at the jungle across the river.

"Hold your fire, everyone. That's an order." Don't know who gave the order. When a squad deploys with a machine gun crew it's called a reinforced squad. Wonder what a squad reinforced with tanks is called. Didn't matter. The pucker was back. Shortly, a young Vietnamese wearing khaki shorts and a black shirt came out of the jungle, his hands clasped behind his head. Someone stated the obvious.

"He's surrendering."

"Sit tight," Sergeant Smith ordered as we all took aim.

Two more Vietnamese appeared in the same posture of surrender. Three more. They all stopped at the river, spread out now looking like they were about to face a firing squad. Which they were. Americans came right behind, poking their M-16s into the backs of our disarmed enemy.

"Move it, move it, move it," we heard distinctly in English. "Get these shorry excuses for sholdiers into that river." Yup. It was Sir Sergeant from Fort Polk. I'd forgotten how much I disliked this pretender. Now I didn't know what to think of him. About midstream he yelled, "Halt!" Holding his rifle in his left hand above the water and pulling a uniformed Vietnamese forward with his right, Sir Sergeant passed everyone until he reached our side. Gruffly, he threw Major Phuoc to the side. "Down," he screamed at Phuoc who went to his knees. "All the way down. On your belly. And keep those hands behind your head."

Sir Sergeant motioned and his patrol brought their prisoners to our shore. In less than a minute all of Phuoc's men lay face down in the dirt in front of the hootches. Sir Sergeant reported to Lieutenant Brown who had made his way to the *al fresco* holding cell. "Sir, thish ish all of 'em 'cept the two dead onesh we left about half a click back."

"Think I'll have that beer now, Coxie," Ty said to his new brother.

"Shaefer, Budweiser? Or, for you mountaineers from the Great Northwest I've got Olympia." Step right up, fellas."

We popped the tops and began sipping. Our mission was complete.

"And now for the koo de grass," Cox said. "Nicky, tell your guys to hold their ears."

The next voice we heard said, "Fire at will!" and the golden minute commenced.

That's how I spent Easter Sunday, 1967.

Chapter 16

Rest and Relaxation

"The reward of a thing well done, is to have done it."
New England Reformers, Ralph Waldo Emerson

We returned to Chu Lai without a Purple Heart among us. Thank you, Lieutenant Troy. The perfunctory field shower felt good while it lasted. But the ritual weapons and ammunition cleaning kept us mindful of the scars we would bear for life. If there is a word to describe the way I for one felt sitting shirtless on my cot, it is "pooped." Sorry, that's the best I can do.

Is this why you never talked about your war, Dad? Does Uncle Pete know anything about what you went through? Does Mom? I started to get angry again at my father, angry because he never shared such an important part of his life that he decided by himself that we should not know about. I was thinking myself into an unnecessary frenzy then thought myself out of it.

Who could I tell back home about the incidents that culminated at Fire Base Bravo? Who would have the patience to listen? Who would believe any of it? Would anyone care?

Wiping bullets and magazine parts in the Tommy proscribed manner I wondered. I wondered why people talked glibly about how soldiering made men of boys. Propaganda. I wondered if I was more manly today than I was a week ago, a month, a year. Had I not been drafted I wondered if I would have reached manhood by now according to somebody's definition. Isn't a United Auto Worker shoveling mud out of grinding machine tubs day after day a man? What about all those "kids" graduating from college and starting careers as teachers, engineers, stock brokers? Forget about that whole other world of girls entering the sisterhood of womanhood.

"Listen up, men." It was Sergeant Smith who had come into the tent. "The Man's giving us all a few days in-country R&R down at Vung Tao."

"Paris of the Orient," Tommy said wistfully.

"That's right, Mr. Hajj," Smith agreed. "We're on our way to Paradise. Thought you might want to catch up on your reading first, though. While we were out, the mailman did cometh."

My brain was too fried to attempt a guess at whatever literary allusion prompted this uncharacteristic turn of a phrase. I knew intuitively it didn't come from anywhere, just Smitty attempting to change our mood. It did. He began ceremoniously handing out letters from the fat stack he pulled out of the side pocket on his fatigues.

"Vladinsky."

"Right over here, Sarge," Eddie said.

"MacDuffy. Hmm," Smith hummed, passing the envelope under his nose while rolling his eyes dreamily. "I think you're going to like this one. And here's one from a Patricia Calloway. Who might this be for?"

"Aunt Patty. Right here." I grabbed it out of his hand before he could get in a tease.

"Come on, Sarge. Where's mine?" Fitzgerald said.

"Patience, my boy. Patience." Sergeant Smith took his sweet time, commenting on what he suspected was in each letter before handing it over. The last one, a thick one, was for PFC Tyrone L. Derkin. "Might Grandmama be trying to slip you a private stash of goodies, Private Derkin?"

"First dibs on them cookies goes to your team leader," McBride says. The rest of us were too busy digesting the personal news from home to think too much about Derkin's care package. At least for the moment.

MacDuffy: "Ah, sure the woman's got impeccable taste in men. She's already planning the wedding. Kiss me, Kate." He planted his pursed lips right smack in the center of the perfumed envelope.

There was more silence in the tent for the next five minutes than in a Trappist monastery during Lent. Smiles all around. No one noticed the tear slide down my cheek. Your father had a stroke at work, Aunt Patty wrote. Your mom's been at the hospital every day and night. She didn't want to worry you, but I thought you needed to know. He's such a good man, Nicky. I've never seen Uncle Pete so upset. You Calloway men don't use the word love very often, but your mother and I know deep down how you feel about each other. I'm so sorry to be the one to give you this terrible news. Forgive me, Nicky.

"Time to fess up, Ty. What did that wee wonderful woman from the Bayou send us?"

"A cook book."

The Vietnamese Riviera

I could go on and on describing the natural beauties of Vietnam. A city kid from Jersey isn't used to all that green, even though it's nickname is The Garden State. And now I was at the shore. The clear water of the South China Sea with its pristine beach was well beyond my ken (I didn't actually know the word pristine at the time, nor ken for that matter).

All I'd ever experienced of seaside resorts until then was the two weeks in July the Calloways, sometimes including Aunt Patty and Uncle Pete, spent each year at honky-tonk Seaside Heights. Too much sun Saturday and Sunday. Mom daubing cold tea bags on my back Sunday night to lift the sting off my sunburned skin that peeled in a few days but never tanned. Board games on the blonde coffee table in the living room of the rented bungalow with linoleum covered floors in every room. And Mom playing the wheels each night on the boardwalk. For her that was better than Bingo every night of the week.

Down the shore, as native Jerseyites put it, we were on vacation. I accepted this annual escape from smog and mosquitoes as a birthright that most of my friends were deprived of. The question never was, are we going down the shore this year? It was simply, when? It's hard to think of myself as having been spoiled as a kid but I guess I was. So be it. Thanks, Mom. Thanks, Dad. I'm going to let you spoil your grandchildren if I'm lucky enough to get out of here.

I'm digressing again, I know, even though I'm getting close to the end of my story. But Vung Tao right now, the idea not the place, was Seaside Heights for the grown up me. The diversions I thought so necessary in my youth, like ferris wheel, carousel, and bumper cars—my favorite to this day—were missing at the far eastern branch of the French Riviera. Those amusements were replaced with morning walks, unhurried conversations, and meals from a menu. Need I mention the bliss that a private bathroom with hot and cold running water provides?

Still, at night we heard bombs bursting in air and could see rockets red glare way off in the distance. Somehow, though, none of that mattered at Vung Tao. The sights and sounds of the war we knew was there didn't evoke ghosts of our recent past. It was more like the Fourth of July. We were on vacation.

The highlight of the four days and three nights—you may not believe this, but it's true, trust me—was Tyrone's perfectly pitched tenor rendition of "Danny Boy," meant specifically for the Fighting Irish, I figured at first, but enjoyed by all the brothers. By the time he reached the second verse he had enchanted us to a faraway land.

> But come ye back when summer's in the meadow,
> Or when the valley's hushed and white with snow.
> I'll be there in sunshine or in shadow;
> Oh, Danny Boy, Oh, Danny Boy, I love you so!

"Where in the holy name of Saint Patrick did that come from," Fitzgerald demanded. "'Tis a gift, for sure." The brogue was not an affectation, rather, the dialect democratized the group.

"'Twas a gift, indeed," says he, "bequeathed to your man from me mammy's side. 'Descendants of Andrew Jackson, we are,' she'd say from time to time. 'And he be descended from Celtic kings, all the ways back to Cuchulain hisself. Don't matter, though, who you come from. What matters is who you become.'"

While I did my tour in Vietnam, 1967, race riots broke out in major cities in the United States. The newspapers called the cities war zones. War zones!

"Are you really related to Andrew Jackson," I asked, prepared to give unconditional acceptance to anything the minstrel said and not having a clue about that Cuchulain guy.

"Don't really know. Don't really care. I'm an American. How 'bout you, Nick?"

"Me, too," I said after a thoughtful pause.

"Me, too, what," Ty pushed.

"Me, too. I'm an American."

Then one by one the brotherhood joined the challenge-response chant.

"Who are you?"

"I'm an American." Loudly. Proudly. "I'm an American."

The army experience, starting back at reception, hadn't exorcised our individuality. Neither had the war. Yet here we were, together, our souls tattooed with the unifying, life defining incidents that forged a collective conscience in each and every one of us at Fire Base Bravo.

While America seemed on the verge of war with itself, again, the unlikeliest fraternity I could have imagined had discovered harmony among ourselves. I finally understood the separate peace Mr. Lyster tried to explain in sixth period sophomore English class. The socioeconomic factors that likely would have divided us as civilians "at home" were inconsequential to the conscripted warriors we had morphed into.

One of the slogans posted in my Latin class read, *Experientia est mater studiorum*, Experience is the mother of learning. How true, how true. I was too smart now, make that too experienced, to allow sunburn to spoil my vacation in Vietnam. That's a start. And although no one, including Mom on her most doting day, would ever have accused me of being overly smart—book smart, anyway—stepping away from the evils of war, even for that little while, I saw and understood the absolute need for peace.

As usually happens when I'm supposed to be getting smart, I get confused. Does one actually have to witness or participate in war in order to recognize its futility? Is that some kind of rule? Why do accidents of birth like race, ethnicity, and religious traditions breed hatred?

I had become a better person in Vietnam, not because of things I did or did not do but because I learned to love. Separation from family brought me closer to them and made me more appreciative of their values. Senseless, man made death instilled in me respect for the sanctity of all life. The Troy patrol taught me that my life finds purpose when it seeks the welfare of others. Most of all, I carry with me to this day the spirit of Jenny 4.

I am my brother's keeper.

Chapter 17

Reunion

"...
In faith and hope the world will disagree,
But all mankind's concern is charity."
An Essay on Man, "Epistle iii, Alexander Pope

Thirty-five years after the formation of the 196th Light Infantry Brigade in 1965, we gathered at the Holiday Inn in New Orleans for a grand reunion. It was my first. Why there? Well, it turns out that the may be/may be not descendant of kings, Mr. Tyrone Derkin, was an officer in the organization and suggested the venue at the last reunion two years earlier. He promised that he could negotiate a great deal on lodging and, further, he offered his personal guarantee that the food would be beyond compare. Ty, you see, was the Master Chef at the place. The aye vote, I'm told, was unanimous.

Jean and I arrived alone, set to enjoy a mini vacation for two school teachers with four children and six grandchildren. Plastered prominently amid the tacky touristy stickers that adorned the back wall of our camper was the one six-year-old PJ bought us for Christmas at his school's Santa's Workshop sale: We're Spending Our Children's Inheritance. Got to love that kid.

So there we were. The sign outside the hotel read: Welcome 196th Chargers. "Oh, wow," Jean said. "They went out of their way to welcome the wives."

"Huh?"

"If your Army buddies are anything like you, Sweetheart, their wives don't let them carry credit cards either."

Wherever we went that weekend, alone or with new old friends, when it came time to pay for something, Good ol' Jean whipped out a stack of credit cards and giggled out louder than necessary, "Charge!"

I had stayed apart too long from these guys, the ones I served with as well as all the others who fought their own dragons after Vietnam. Harboring survivor's guilt for a long time, I suppressed the more important, positive lessons of self-discovery: caring, trusting, and loving. I suffered from depression and didn't know it. Yeah, you're right, I probably knew it but wouldn't admit it. I was too tough, too self-assured, too sane. Anyway, I felt down in the dumps more often than I should have.

I proposed to Jean, beautiful, intelligent, and, yes, witty Jean. "Please say yes," I prayed.

"Yes."

Whew!

"But I need you to do something."

"Anything."

"I love you, Nicky. You know that. I don't want anything to come between us."

"Nothing will ever . . ."

"Hear me out," she said in a voice I hadn't heard before. "You are the most wonderful man I have ever met or hope to meet. I am ready to give myself to you. All of me."

"Jean . . ."

"Shhh!" Her tone softened as she took my hands in hers and looked straight into my eyes. "I know you love me, Nick." Deep breath. "I don't know how big it is, but there is a part of you that you won't share. Maybe you think you can't. You need to get it out. You need help."

I made a lame attempt at joking my way out with a line Macbeth used in defending his manhood to his would be queen, Lady Macbeth. "Prithee, peace: I dare do all that may become a man; Who dares do more is none."

"Don't hide behind Shakespeare, Nick. But if you must, let me put it this way. I'm looking forward to a long, long love poem of a life with you, not a tragedy. And by the way, your buddy Macbeth had it wrong. What's done *can* be undone. Or at least what's done can be unraveled enough to make you free to love and be loved, totally. No strings. No baggage."

And so I went to therapy thirty years ago. And so Jean and I are sleeping on a king size bed this weekend in an air conditioned room instead of a camper, sharing the company of about three hundred or so other middle aged couples swapping photos of kids and grandkids, buying voodoo trinkets and tee shirts on Bourbon Street for the grandchildren.

The banquet Saturday night surpassed all expectations. I had told Jean Ty's little lie of a secret about being a cook in the army. "Worked like a leprechaun's charm," he said with a devilish grin. "Mom still don't know the truth. And you don't be tellin' her, neither. Ain't nobody in N'Orleans know nothin' but I was fixin' up mountains of Creole dishes for you grunts over there in, where was it, oh, yeah, over there in Vietnam." He pronounced "nam" like "yam."

"Why, Mr. Derkin," Jean flirted. "You are just about the lowdowndest twig of the Andrew Jackson family tree I ever did set my eyes upon."

"I thank you, ma'am. I thank you kindly."

"But my word, you sure can cook. Tell me, though, gourmet to gourmand, did ye be taking the overalls out of Mrs. Murphy's pot before stirring in the chowder?"

"'Tis an Irish trick, it's true," he flirted right back at her. "Adds that special flavor, Lassie. And softens the crayfishes' fall when I tosses the little darlin' beggars in."

"It will remain our little secret, Mr. Derkin."

"Thank you kindly, Mrs. Calloway."

That's about the way most of the socializing went that night. Small talk, silly talk, getting to know you kind of talk. I'd almost forgotten that Sergeant Smith, Smitty, had a first name. Leonard. "Lenny," he said by way of introducing himself to Jean.

"So pleased to meet you, Lenny," Jean said. "You're one of the good guys Nicky has told me so much about."

"They're all good guys, Jean. Every last one of them."

Lenny re-upped after Vietnam, went back in '69 with the 1st Cavalry. "Wasn't the same as with the 196th, though. The Cav was good, no doubt about it. But I couldn't get as close to the men as I could with you guys, Nick. Had too much rank. Spent most of my second tour in base camp saying 'Yes, Sir, no, Sir,'" while the young bucks were getting shot at in the boonies."

"You went back?"

"Yeah. Hey, that's enough of that. We're here to have a good time."

Lenny played guide. He offered that he had been married for a few years. No kids. "The divorce was my fault, mostly. Guess I wasn't the settling down type. She still sends a card on my birthday. Never misses. Hitched up with a dentist. Nice guy."

The hall brimmed with happy people. The partyers in the corner stood out. Seemingly oblivious to all around them, the tam o'shantered Fighting Irismen and their spouses were intermingled arm in arm with Clan Derkin. Mrs. Derkin, Ty's mom, was leading the chorus as we neared them.

"H-A-double R-I-G-A-N spells Harrigan."

"Harrigan," they shouted out in refrain hitting different notes but nobody cared.

"That's the name that no shame ever has been connected with: Harrigan, that's me."

"Whoa! Whoa! Nicky Calloway, me boy. Gitchyer arse over here and give us a hug."

Startled just a bit that the unmistakable Sean McDuffy recognized me, I let go of Jean's hand, preparing to greet the balding Mick with a paunch. I'd have to wait for our hug. Mrs. Derkin grabbed Mac's sleeve and jerked him down to where his ear was near her mouth but not so close as to deprive us all from the bogus balling out he was about to receive.

"We don't use that foul language 'round here, boy. If you are referring to Mr. Calloway's bottom, then you say 'bottom.' If you are referring to Mr. Calloway's donkey, you may say 'arse.'" She let go of his sleeve and wagged her best schoolmarm finger an inch from his nose. "Hear?"

"Right on, Mrs. Derkin," Fitzgerald cheered. "You tell him."

"You'll have to be forgivin' 'im," says Paddy McBride. "His people come from the County Cork, ya know."

"Right y'are, Missus," Big Sean apologized without the slightest hint of sincerity. "Now, Nickey, getcher big fat donkey over here."

They hadn't changed. And the Derkins played right along with a jaunting carload of their own blarney. "We've a straight line back to the Great Cuchulain himself," Uncle Muhammed in his bright blue with silver trim dashiki told Jean and me later. He didn't bother with the brogue thing.

Jean ate it up. "You must be so proud," she said. "Why, I'll just bet a pot o' gold that if that Andy Jackson feller were here right now he'd be leading the Siege of Ennis right out on that dance floor."

The reunion was a time for joy. A time to reflect. For me, a time to heal. The one guy I really wanted Jean to meet couldn't make it. Tommy Hajj is a counselor at a crisis center in Philadelphia, Lenny told us. He and his wife, Tabitha, sent in their confirmation but he called on Friday to say that "something had come up at work." Jean asked me to promise we would get to Philadelphia as soon as we could. She pressed.

"Call him tomorrow, Nick. Lenny has his number."

(We stopped at Philly on the way back to Jersey and had dinner with Tommy and Tabitha the following Wednesday night. He's doing fine. She's a nurse at a teaching hospital. They have four children. We're going to stay in touch.)

Lenny led us away from Hibernia Corner. "Some more folks you have to say Hi to." As he led Jean and me across the crowded ballroom, he prepared me, although I wasn't prepared enough when we got there. "Joe Troy, this is . . ."

"Nick! Great to see you. This is my third reunion. I ask every time, 'Did Nick Calloway register?' So glad you finally made it."

Rising slowly from his chair as Joe Troy introduced Jean and me to his family was a man I did not recognize. He looked older than most of the guys, too old to be a grunt Charger, I thought. Maybe it was the walker behind his chair that threw me off.

"Nick Calloway, this is one of my best friends, Paul Richardson. Paul, say hello to my brother, Nick."

To this day I can't remember much less describe the range of emotions that overwhelmed me. I think I even puckered. I had told Jean what a great man Lieutenant Troy was and that I hoped she'd get to meet him. I told my therapist but never Jean about Fire Base Bravo. Richardson was a name she could not associate with the pastel image I had painted for her of my time in Vietnam.

Dr. Mensana agreed with me that inflicting gory details on Jean would serve no healthy purpose for her or for me. The most important thing, "critical," he said, was for me to report the story to him. "Get it out." At our final session the good doctor whom I did not want to trust in the beginning said something like this: "Nick, all those things that happened in Vietnam happened. You cannot change them. It is your attitude about them that must change, and you have made considerable progress in doing that since you came to me six months ago. Your depression is not a sickness, it is a wound."

Never patronizing, Dr. Mensana likened my condition to that of a cardiac patient. He made it personal. "Your father's stroke occurred because of congenitally flawed arteries, Nick. The condition was hidden from him. It could have killed him but it did not; the stroke was your father's wake-up call." He reminded me of things I had told him about Dad's battle back to a decent life. "After the stroke, I'll make an educated guess, your father felt depressed. Understandable, wouldn't you say?"

"Yes."

"Yes. He could have succumbed to the 'why me' syndrome and spent the rest of his life feeling sorry for himself."

"He did not." I was adamant.

"No, Nick, he did not. He fought. He continues to fight valiantly against an enemy he did not choose. Plaque crept into his cardiovascular system, ambushed him, nearly struck a fatal blow. From what you have told me his most powerful weapons are his change in diet and daily exercise. Yes?"

"Yes."

"Tell me, Nick. Who prepares your father's meals?"

"Mom."

"Who walks with your father every night?"

"His brother Pete."

"Who takes him to physical therapy twice each week?"

"I do."

"You see, Nick, your father's return to health is primarily his own responsibility. It is his choice to eat right and exercise. Or not. And he gets plenty of help and support from people who love him. Do you feel burdened when you take your father to his therapy and have to sit for an hour or two in the waiting room at night when you could be doing something else?"

"No. Absolutely not."

"Absolutely not. You love your father, as do your mother and uncle. Another educated guess: participating in your father's rehabilitation, contributing to his quality of life, these things make you feel pretty good."

"Yes. They do. I only wish I could do more."

"Nick, you must allow others to do the same for you.

Oh, boy. Talk about digressions. I'm going to rationalize this particular story board tangent to a healthy mind. Although you may not agree, I like to think that Dr. Mensana would. Your choice. Like it or not, though, since you're still with me, I'm going to consider you a friend I just haven't met yet. Before I go on, then, I want to thank you for bearing with me this far.

It's none of my business how Joe and Paul found each other after the war and became such good friends. Whatever. There they were, their families sitting comfortably together, adult children reminiscing like the old friends they were. Marianne Troy introduced her three late twenty-something children: Marianne, a carbon copy of her beautiful mother, who was with her husband, Dan; Li and Lee, woman and man of Oriental extraction. "It was always easier when I called the kids to dinner," Marianne joked.

Corrine Richardson introduced their two sons and their wives. "This is Paschal and his wife Sandy." I learned later that Paschal was born on Easter Sunday, 1967. "And this is Charles and his wife Honey." Corrine and Paul had adopted Charles, a Vietnamese refugee, who loathed being called Charley.

My mind raced all through dinner. Hope my silence didn't insult anyone at the table. Jean, always the more gregarious partner in the relationship, held up the Calloway end of the table talk. "Oh, we met at a five mile race at a teachers convention in Atlantic City."

"Runners!"

"Actually, no," she admitted with candid self deprecation. "It was at the water stop at mile four. Remember, Nick?"

I remembered. She'd told the story a thousand times.

"We were near the end of the pack . . ."

"We were the end of the pack," I interrupted, as she knew I would.

"Anyway," she continued, "we didn't jog by the table and toss down a cup on the run like real runners do, you know, the ones who glance at their watches to check their time. Not Nicky and me. We stopped and chugged two cups of water. And then—this is the good part . . ."

She had enthralled her thousand and first audience. "And then," Eddie's wife, Marcia, asked.

"Well, and then I grabbed another two cups and let him have both barrels. I threw the water into his face. 'Looks like you needed that, slow poke,' I laughed, and ran away." She turned to me mockingly, as though we were alone. "You looked sooo cute, Nicky, standing there in your yellow nylon shorts and bright red face."

I blushed. Happens every time.

"Nicky, you're sooo cute," she whispered loud enough for all to hear.

"May I have your attenshion, please." My back was to the head table but there was no mistaking that voice. "Thank you." Sir Sergeant from Fort Polk's lisp no longer grated my ears, that sensation having been expunged at Fire Base Bravo. He carried on effortlessly with the program. We heard remarks from a retired sergeant major and a retired general, who commanded a 196th company in 1969 as a captain, and the current commander of the 196th, a reserve unit stationed in Hawaii attached to the 25th Infantry Division as a training brigade. Sir Sergeant—Mike Jenkins—invited Joe Troy to the podium.

I found it difficult thinking of the Ranger, my first hero, as "Joe," much less calling him anything other than "Sir" or "Lieutenant Troy."

Joe's job was to introduce our guest speaker, "a man," he said, "whom most of you don't know. He is the most fascinating man I ever met," he said. "Those of us who served with him called him "Captain" out of the respect he earned. He was the interpreter for Alpha Company, 3-2-1 in 1967.

Joe provided a biographical sketch before and after, not during, the war. Jean took my hand in both of hers and rested the tacit, tangible symbol of our love in her lap. She knew the man I called "an angel."

JENNY 4

"American soldiers have always held dear and lived the principles of Honor, Duty, Country," Joe said, as he related those words to Captain Thuoc, retaining this appellation of respect. "Soldiers today are also guided by the mnemonic LDRSHIP." Again, he gave illustrations of how Captain Thuoc led his entire life as a personification of the code: Leadership, Duty, Respect, Selfless Service, Honor, Integrity, Personal Courage.

Jean clasped my hand tighter and rubbed the back of it tenderly. The hairs on my arm tingling.

"Please join me in giving a Chargers welcome to our brother, Master, Nguyen Thuoc."

He stood before us, head bowed, until finally he said, "Please, my friends. Please be seated." His voice was clear but soft. Even now, especially now, his presence comforted me. He spoke without notes, his words flowing from his soul, as they always had.

"You fine men come to my country not in search of personal glory," he said. "You come to my country because we are a people in need. Lieutenant Richardson kindly call me a humble man. I am sorry, Sir, I do not find it easy to call you Joe in front of your comrades." He shrugged one shoulder as if to say, "What are you going to do? I have the microphone."

"I am not a humble man. I am a humbled man. This is my first visit to America. I am your guest. Last week, I go to Washington with Joe and Marianne Troy." He pronounced Joe with two syllables—Jo oh—which drew a subdued laugh from the crowd. "I see The Wall." Quiet in the room.

"So many American boys give their lives for me, an old man now. So many boys give their lives for my country. I am humbled by your sacrifice. Please permit me to say the words Joe say to me when I arrive in San Francisco: Welcome home!"

The Fighting Irishmen jumped out of their chairs and started the standing ovation. The humble man stood proudly with head held high. While we stood clapping and clapping, whistling and cheering, he walked slowly across the parquet dance floor, close enough to the tables for us to hear his final words. We remained on our feet.

"My brothers and sisters . . ."

Silence in the room.

Nguyen Thuoc extended his arms laterally several inches from his sides, faced the palms of his hands toward us, and said reverently, "Peace be with you."